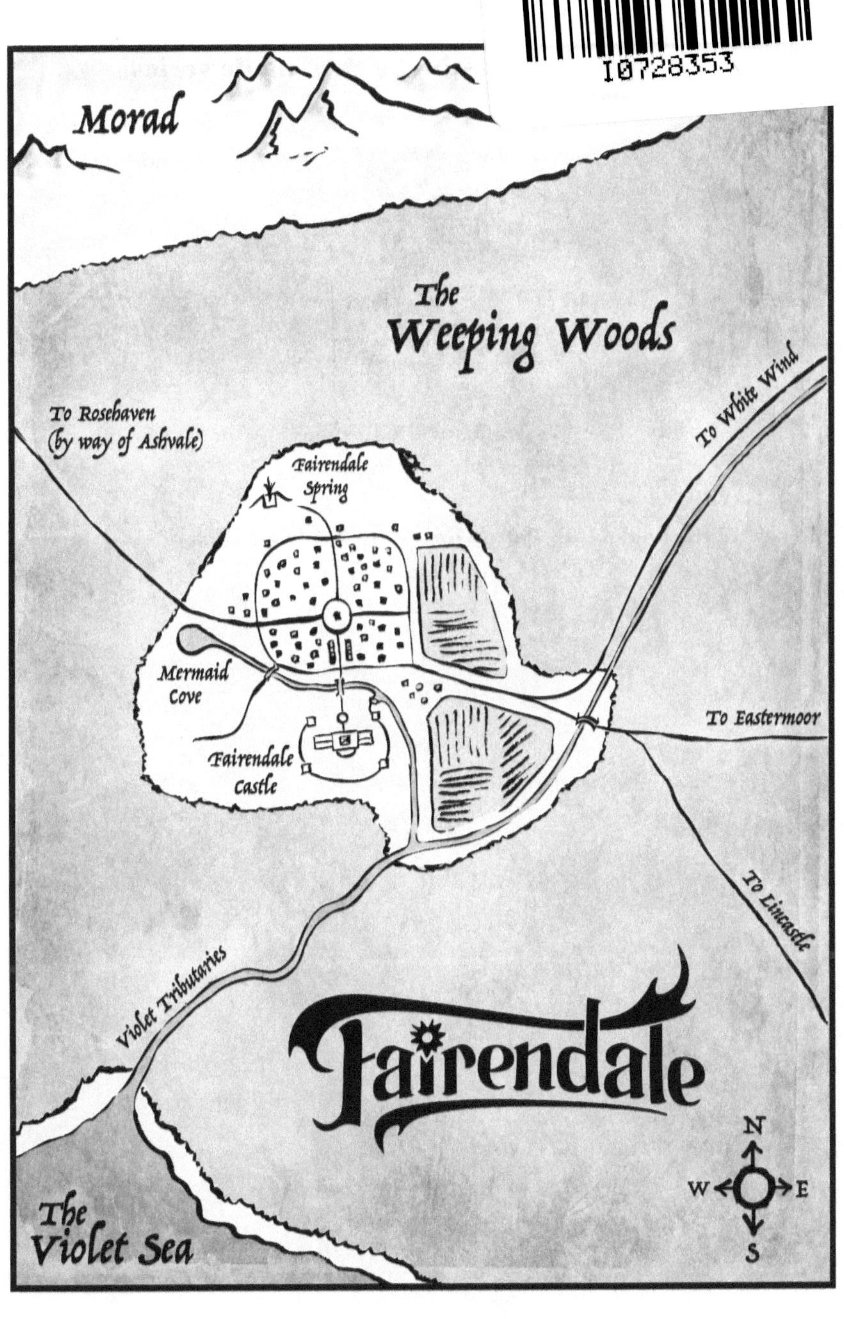

Morad
The Weeping Woods
To Rosehaven
(by way of Ashvale)
To White Wind
Fairendale Spring
Mermaid Cove
Fairendale Castle
To Eastermoor
To Lincastle
Violet Tributaries
Fairendale
The Violet Sea
N
W E
S
I0728353

Read all the books in the Fairendale series!

Book .5: *The Good King's Fall (a prequel)*
Book 1: *The Treacherous Secret*
Book 2: *The King's Pursuit*
Book 3: *The Perilous Crossing*
Book 4: *The Dragons of Morad*
Book 5: *The Fiery Aftermath*
Book 6: *The Mysterious Separation*

Collector's Editions:
Books 1-6: *The Flight of the Magical Children*

To see all the books L.R. Patton has written, please click or visit the link below:

www.lrpatton.com/store

Fairendale

5

THE FIERY AFTERMATH

Batlee Press
PO Box 591596
San Antonio, TX 78259

Printed in the United States of America

First Edition—2016/Cover designed by Toalson Marketing
www.toalsonmarketing.com

L.R. PATTON

THE FIERY AFTERMATH

BATLEE
PRESS

*To the ones
who are brave enough
to try*

Time

Cora stands in the middle of the village, staring at the houses around her, wondering how many of them are still inhabited and how many have been abandoned, now that she has begun making her plans, now that she has called the people to action, now that she has put the idea in their heads. She wonders how many of the village people are cowards, like her father was, how many of them must have stolen away in the dark of night so they will not have to join the dangerous quest to release the children, though the villagers are still only in the strengthening time of the plan and have quite some way to go before the attacking time. But they know what is coming. They have seen her plans, after all.

It is late afternoon, and not a soul has stepped from their houses, though there is plenty to see.

Cora looks up. Flames draw closer. She watches them leap

toward the sky and then die back down. The woods have begun burning, those Weeping Woods that have not seen a burning like this one since King Sebastien stole Fairendale's throne. She has heard of that burning in stories, the burning done by the dragons, after which all the trees magically lived and soon bore their green once more, but, for a time, wore their black like mourning rags. That is, in fact, why the woods are called the Weeping Woods. And now it is burning again. Because of dragons. It was said that the dragons did not remain in the land after the Great Battle, but Cora knows they did, for she knows many things others do not.

Cora feels a smile playing at the corners of her lips.

Yes. She knows they remain.

In the case of dragons awakening, perhaps she will not be the only one to wage war against the castle. Perhaps the people of Fairendale will have the unlikeliest of allies—dragons that people have not seen for far too long.

The first time she saw a dragon was long ago, when she flew the sky wearing her second skin. No one could do transformation the way she could. Shape shifting was not the normal way of magic, of course. It was only the way of dark magic joining with the light, a magic gift bestowed on only a few at birth. She could control both. Not many could, which is why the realm was not said to be home to many shape shifters. She had done it often as a girl, but, alas, her daughter had not inherited the gift.

Perhaps Mercy would be alive now if she had.

Cora, when a girl, would soar over the dragon lands, but the dragons stayed well hidden from an untrained eye. She caught sight of one only once. Its eyes followed her movements, and she had wondered, momentarily, if dragons feasted on birds or whether she was too small a target to even bother with the chase. The dragon must have thought so, for he let her be, and she never ventured over the dragon lands again. They were too dangerous.

But perhaps the people will see dragons again. Perhaps the people will be able to live in harmony with the dragons, as they had done in King Brendon's day. Perhaps she and the rest of the people can restore Fairendale to its former glory. She had never, in truth, seen the kingdom in its former glory, for she was not born in the days of King Brendon. But the stories tell of its beauty.

Cora hears a door open on one of the houses behind her. She turns. A man steps from it. The baker. She thought surely he had left, since she had seen no movement since the day she had called them all inside the secret underground chamber that lies beneath the village fountain and laid out her plans. Yet he is still here. He does not see her, though. His face is turned toward the woods.

Another door opens. An old woman emerges. She looks at Cora, and then she looks toward the woods. Another and another and another step from their homes, more than Cora thought possible, and they all stand in the streets with their faces toward the woods.

It burns at an alarming rate. The trees set off a great light, greater even than the day, for the sun is nowhere to be found. The heat curls over them and warms them better than their threadbare blankets. They are, perhaps, glad for this fire, for they do not have to shiver as they have done all night.

The people stand watching, in a silence that is heavier than the day's sky. And then Cora says, "Dragons," and the people look at her. They widen their eyes. She sees their fear. So she laughs. "There is no need to be afraid," she says. "They will not hurt us. Their quarrel is with the castle, not with us."

The people do not question how Cora might know something such as this. They would not believe her, of course, if she were to tell them. They would not believe that she had worn the feathers of a bird moments before she stood in the middle of the streets, for Cora has a magical child. Cora passed her magic on. Cora should have nothing left.

But what many people do not know about shape shifters is that their shape-shifting magic remains with them, though they can do no other magic. So it is that Cora, at the first sight of flame, donned her animal robe and took to the sky. She saw the great multitude of dragons. She saw the king's men, fallen throughout the land. She saw the dead horses.

She did not, however, see any children.

The king's men, it seems, crossed too far into the dragon lands. Cora feels the triumph warming her throat as the fire draws near enough to warm her face. The dragons will come for the king, if fortune remains on the side of the people.

And if the dragons do not come, the castle will be without its guard. It will be vulnerable. It will be all too easy to steal inside and release the children.

Cora turns to the villagers. "People of Fairendale," she says. They look at her, their eyes no longer fearful. "The king's men have perished." She waves toward the flames, flickering closer. "Because of the dragons." Once again, no one questions how she knows information like this. Cora has always been an outcast among the people, for she was known to have deep, dark magic back when she was a girl. And it is true that she passed that magic on to her daughter, and her daughter had no trouble making friends here. But let us not dwell on that. Let us see Cora, as she stands today, the wind flapping through her blood-red hair, whipping it about her face. She brushes it aside, so the people might see the glow of her green eyes.

A woman, you see, does not need friends to lead. She merely needs authority. And this woman's words, her way of speaking, give her authority.

Cora smiles at all the people, who seem to have handed her their blind trust now. It was not always so. Perhaps it takes great tragedy to show people what needs doing. So there is some good that comes from evil. Perhaps one merely has to look in the right place to find the good.

"What this means for us," Cora says, "is that the castle is vulnerable."

The people murmur around her, as if understanding, now, what she means and what they must do. And then the baker, good man, grins at her. "So what shall we do?" he says, though it is plain to see that he knows.

"We shall attack," Cora says. "Tomorrow night."

"And what of this night?" a man from the back calls out. "Will the king not be most vulnerable tonight?"

"Let the king feel his fear," Cora says. "Let him feel his vulnerability. Let it shake his bones and keep him from his sleep." Cora breathes long and deep. "And then we shall attack."

The people nod. She is respected now as their leader, for no one else took it upon themselves to do what she has done. They will do anything she says now.

"Tonight," Cora tells them, "we shall meet in the secret

chamber, and we shall make our plans."

"But what of the fire?" a woman says. The people lift their eyes toward the blaze.

Cora stares at it, too. The fire did not touch the village last time. It will not touch it now. "We need not worry," Cora says. "It will give us warmth for a time. We must permit it." For she knows, dear reader, that there are colder days ahead.

So the people file back inside their houses to watch the burning from their windows, for the air outside is full of death and smoke and silence.

Cora remains in the street. She lifts her face to the sky, roiling with clouds that are not clouds at all, and lifts her hands to the warmth. The hot breath hits her face, and she remembers, now, the words that an old prophetess told her once upon a time. Fire, the prophetess had said, is sometimes needed to clear away unnecessary pieces and reveal what lies within.

So she watches the fire burn, unafraid of its wrath.

"So," the great dragon Zorag says. He stands on top of a mountain, at the mouth of a cave. "So there is you."

He is the only dragon on this mountain. Except for his cousin, that is, hanging about in the shadows where not even

Zorag can see him. Blindell is his name. He is not nearly so massive at Zorag, for he is a young dragon, having lived only about half as long as his cousin and yet longer, now, than his parents.

Arthur, you might be surprised to know, is alive. He is huddled, even now, in this damp cave. He is a prisoner of the dragons, bound by the laws of this land. He is given water and meat and nothing more. The meat the dragons scorch first with a burst of fire from their mouths. It is a source of comic entertainment for them, for they eat meat raw and find it odd that one would eat it blackened. Though one might argue that people do not eat it blackened either. But, alas, this is beyond the understanding of dragons.

"So there is me," Arthur says. He has not withered as yet. He is not afraid of dragons, for he knew one once. "And what do you want of me?"

He has asked this question of many other dragons, ones who have carried him to water, a small tributary of the Violet Sea that runs through the desert land, in their jaws and then carried him back. But none can answer.

This is the first time he has seen Zorag since the fiery battle last morn. Zorag remains mostly with his dragons, settling them, advising them, ordering them to have patience, for it is not yet the time for attack. They must see what happens next. They must determine whether there is another danger coming for them.

The dragons want nothing more than revenge for the breach of a treaty, agreed upon long ago. Zorag maintains that they have seen their revenge, for not a man lived through the battle. Arthur excepted, of course. Mysteriously, all of the bodies vanished moments ago. Not one of them remains. No one has been able to explain it. But if one were to travel back in time to the days of the Great Battle and, more recently, the Roundup, one would marvel at how very similar these battlegrounds ended up: empty of all bodies and evidence that a battle had ever taken place.

The dragons, too, have been asking about the man Zorag keeps in a cave. Is he a pet? Is he a bargaining chip? Is he their food, for he will not feed many. He is too wispy, they say.

One might agree that one human would not provide much food at all for the fifty-three dragons in this land.

Fifty-three dragons, you might say? How have they remained hidden all these years? Well, you see, dragons, as we have mentioned before, are very good at hiding. Their colors change, blending with their background. When they close their eyes, they nearly disappear altogether.

Truth be told, Zorag does not quite know what he wants of Arthur yet. He only knows that the man reminds him of someone he once knew and loved, a man with a good heart, a man whom he would sometimes carry on his back and take for a flight out in the hills, where they could not be seen by anyone other than the animals of the fields. This is why Zorag has kept Arthur alive. This is why Zorag let the others, whom we know as Maude and the children, go, for he did not lose any of the humans who crossed into his land. He merely turned away.

Zorag, you see, has a good heart. He heard this man's plea, and he looked on the children, sensing their fear, and because he still remembers the joy he used to feel in the days of old, days when he played with the children of the kingdom freely and they played freely with the dragons, he could not destroy the ones who stood before him. So much as a serpent's heart can be turned toward pity, so was Zorag's. In the very moment the king's men crossed into Morad, Zorag sent the silent message to his dragons, calling for an attack on the king's men, but adding that they must let the children and the woman go. He had watched the group tear toward a cave on the perimeter of the woods, where he knew they would be safe.

Of course the dragons had known for some time that the man and the woman and all the children were walking about their lands. Zorag had held his people at bay, hoping the intruders would be gone before too very long. Instead, they had brought more intruders.

Zorag grieves for the land. He grieves for the forest. He mostly grieves for all the people who were killed in the battle. This is not the way it is supposed to go. If only the king's men had remained on their side of the line. If only they had honored the treaty. If only the dragons had let them go.

If he could do it all again, Zorag would have warned the men away. But our kind dragon knows as well as we do: time does not turn back but only marches forward.

And so Zorag stands on the brink of a cave, where a man steps into the fading light.

"I want nothing of you," Zorag says, looking out across the dragons that now move about freely. For years they have kept their existence a secret. Now they freely roam. There is no need for the secrecy now that the forest burns. Anyone would know it burned because of dragons.

But the dragons cannot roam far enough. Morad, you see, is running out of food. Every night, the one on food duty must journey farther and farther into the other kingdoms to try to find enough sustenance to keep the dragons alive. The dragons grow hungrier by the day. Zorag has run out of ideas.

"I am here for a reason," Arthur says. "Am I not?"

Zorag turns away from the dragons and back to Arthur. That face. Unfamiliar. And yet those eyes. He has seen those eyes somewhere before. Long ago, perhaps. "You are here because you broke the treaty.”

“No,” Arthur says. “That is not why I am here.”

And he is right, dear reader, though Zorag cannot point to the exact reason he has kept this man. Perhaps because of the familiar eyes? Perhaps for the purpose of working out a plan to save the dragons, as he had once saved a man? Perhaps to restore the kingdom to what it once was? Could this man be their only hope?

This is dangerous thinking, even for a dragon as powerful as Zorag. Restoring the kingdom will mean war, and his dragons are far too weak for war. The last one…

“What are you called?” Zorag says.

“I am Arthur of Fairendale,” Arthur says.

“Arthur,” Zorag says. “You remind me of someone I once knew.”

“And you remind me of a dragon I once knew,” Arthur says. His voice is genuine, soft. Zorag turns away, back to the dragons. “I knew a dragon once who was brave and kind and fought for the good of the people.”

“I have never fought for the good of the people,” Zorag says, though it is not true. He remembers the battle well, though he does not want to. He lost both his parents in that battle, as had Blindell. And after it, he had taken over the care of his cousin and all the dragons had hidden from the king who did not shudder to slay a dragon.

He would like very much to forget all that. He would like very much to forget that he ever had a rider, that his rider had ever disappeared.

"I think you once loved a rider," Arthur says, for he can see the sadness drawn upon Zorag's face.

Zorag growls at him. "You know nothing," he says.

Arthur dips his head. "I know nothing," he says. "But I see." He lifts his head again and stares into Zorag's eyes. Zorag cannot look away from Arthur, as if Arthur has woven some kind of spell around them, a spell where Zorag can hear the voice of his past calling to him, begging him for help. Is Arthur reading his mind? Does he have that kind of magic? It is impossible to tell.

Finally, Arthur lets him go, and Zorag does not waste any time in backing away.

"There is a battle going on in the kingdom of Fairendale," Arthur says.

"Men and their battles," Zorag says. "They are none of our concern."

"Men and their battles," Arthur says. He is quiet for some moments, before he says, "Except this one is over children." He looks out across the land of the dragons, out toward the forest that burns still. "This one is over my children."

"What do men want of children?" Zorag says.

"Everything," Arthur says, "when the children are magical ones."

Zorag knows nothing of this world, magic and men. He knows only of dragons and their powers that are so much greater than those of men, and their one weakness, the place where the scales and head meet, the very place the warrior who stormed The Good King Brendon's castle years ago seemed to know about. That man's army had perfect aim all those years ago. Might that have been magic as well?

"We have our own battle to fight," Zorag says.

Arthur turns to him and looks on the dragon with deep sadness brimming in his eyes, as if he cares about this, too. Of course Zorag chose a kind man to keep. This was the way of things. They were always harder to kill.

"And what battle is yours?" Arthur says.

"People," Zorag says. "They are hunting us."

"Why would people hunt dragons?" Arthur says, as if he cannot comprehend a single reason.

Perhaps we can help him, dear reader. Dragons are dangerous. Dragons are powerful. Dragons are mysteriously beautiful. The skins of dragons are worth fortunes in other kingdoms, though Fairendale was never one to welcome the wearing of scales.

"We are starving," Zorag says. "We must find food."

"So you find it in other lands?" Arthur says.

Zorag spits a long ray of fire. "Lands other than Fairendale."

"But the woods have animals yet," Arthur says.

Zorag growls. "Dragons keep treaties. We were told not to cross the line. So we did not."

"So you hunt in other places," Arthur says.

Zorag merely growls.

"And the people now want to hunt you," Arthur says. "Because you are taking their food."

They are quiet for some time. And then Arthur dares place a hand on the dragon's front leg. Zorag roars at him, and Arthur backs away. "I only thought—" he says.

Zorag roars again. The pain, you see, has become too much. It is not a pain of his body but a pain of his heart, and it beats and beats and beats until he can do nothing but roar.

The head of every dragon in the land turns his way.

By the time he is finished, Arthur is weeping. He did not know, you see, that before him stood a dragon with a pain so deep and wide and long that it is nearly unbearable.

After a time, Zorag grows quiet. So Arthur risks. "Perhaps we might help each other," he says.

Zorag raises his yellow eyes to Arthur's. The orange flecks within them shimmer. "And how would you be able to help me?"

Zorag says. He spits another long stream of fire. Arthur senses that the dragon has become angry.

"Our battle is over innocent children," Arthur says. "Your battle is over the innocent need to feed your people. We are both right. We are both justified."

"There is nothing we can do," Zorag says. "I am no longer a war dragon."

"But you once were?" Arthur says.

And here is the exact moment when Zorag's cousin slides from the shadows. Arthur is frightened at first by this dragon's endless spikes, spikes on his head, spikes on his wings, spikes on his legs and his sides and his back, as if he is made of a thousand spikes that wait to cut through the skin of a person. This is a dangerous dragon, blue-black like the midnight sky. His eyes glow red.

"Cousin was a great warrior," the dragon hisses.

Zorag turns on the dragon. "You should not be here, Blindell," he says.

"I thought I might help," Blindell says.

"You should not be here," Zorag says.

"I was only listening," Blindell says. "Listening to a dragon talk with a man." He glares at his cousin. Zorag turns his head away.

"My cousin," Zorag says, to no one in particular, "lost his

parents in the Great Battle, as did I."

"I watched Zorag fight," Blindell says. "He was magnificent." He looks at Arthur, his eyes like the poppies Maude planted outside their door in the village.

Oh, Maude. How he misses her.

"He could be magnificent again," Blindell says.

"I do not ask him to be magnificent," Arthur says. "I merely ask for help."

"Dragons do not help men," Zorag says. "Men fixed that for us long ago."

"But perhaps," Blindell says, "this man is right. Perhaps we could help each other."

Zorag shakes his magnificent head. "No," he roars. "You should not be here, Blindell."

"Cousin," Blindell says.

"Go," Zorag says. "You are not welcome here." They stare at one another, and then Blindell lifts into the sky.

If one were to dip inside the mind of Blindell for just a moment, one would see that he does not like leaving, but he will. For now. He will also tell the others. He knows what they will want to do, and together they shall convince his cousin that they must join forces with the man and finally, after so many years, do something. He will get what he wants. Revenge.

Arthur watches the shadow dragon disappear into the night

and shivers, just once. Then he faces Zorag. "If you are not going to help the children," he says. "Then I must."

"You must remain here," Zorag says. "You are going nowhere."

"Please," Arthur says. "Please let me help the children."

Zorag roars, fire streaming from his mouth and lighting the night sky. He turns his face toward Arthur, but he does not burn him. Then he lifts into the sky on his massive wings and spreads the flashing fire wherever he goes.

Arthur huddles in a corner of the cave and waits.

There will be a moment. He must bide his time.

Rider

Many years before this one, the dragons of Morad were largely ignored by the people of Fairendale, though the people knew of their existence. When reminded of the existence of dragons so near them, on the other side of the Weeping Woods, the people of Fairendale considered their presence with great suspicion and fear. Such large beings would be hard to look upon without suspicion and fear. But, for the most part, the dragons and the people lived out their lives in two separate places. There was no love between them, though there was no animosity, either.

This is the world Zorag was born into.

One hundred forty-two years ago, Zorag was born on a stormy night, to a mother and father who ruled the lands of Morad. He did not know of people until a day when he flew too close to the village and saw them running back into their houses.

He asked his parents about them when he returned from his flight.

"We try not to fly over the village of Fairendale," his father said. "The people are afraid of us."

"Why are the people afraid of us?" Zorag said. "I did not wish to hurt them."

"They do not understand us," his mother said. "So we try to stay out of their way."

But Zorag was curious about the people, who looked so different than his own. At first he saved his flying for night, but the people were not out and about then. So he ventured closer and closer to the village throughout the day, circling the sky but giving no indication that he would land. He did not wish to frighten the people, after all.

It did not take him long to find the castle. With its large towers, pointing toward the sky, and its extravagant size, it was quite difficult to miss. He wondered what sort of people lived inside. He returned again and again, until he found a boy, standing on the steps.

Something about the boy pulled him to the ground. Zorag was not yet fully grown at the time, and so he was not so large as dragons could get. The boy did not run when he landed before him.

"Hello," the boy said.

And Zorag realized he could speak to the boy. "Hello," he said.

"I have never seen a dragon up close," the boy said. He moved closer. "My father says you are dangerous."

"We are not dangerous," Zorag said. "We do not wish to hurt you."

"I know," the boy said. "I have known all along."

Zorag liked this boy. And this is what made him say, "I am called Zorag."

"I am called Brendon." The boy touched his skin. Zorag felt a recognition trigger in him, though he could not say why. Dragons, you see, know when they have found their riders. But they do not know enough to say.

Zorag only knew that when Brendon said, "May I climb on your back?" he did not hesitate to say, yes, he could. He did not hesitate to lift into the sky with the boy. He did not hesitate to fly over the village and the dragon lands with a rider on his back.

No one knew of their secret, at least not until Brendon became king. He understood the dragons so well by the time he inherited the throne that he urged his people to live in harmony with them. He knew, you see, that his people needed dragons as much as the dragons needed his people.

And so began their partnership.

The dragons were used mostly for transportation, by the

soldiers of the kingdom who were often gone on peace-keeping journeys. In those days, the kingdom of Fairendale was in no danger at all, for all the lands had heard of the dragons and the people joining forces. No man wanted to attack a land populated with dragons.

Over time, the dragons and the people became friends.

King Brendon no longer rode Zorag, for Zorag's father, Erell, became the king's dragon. Zorag never told his father about the recognition he had felt when King Brendon, before he was king, touched him. His father would not have understood. Erell was the king of the dragons. He believed he should protect the king of Fairendale. And so Zorag said goodbye to his rider and waited for another.

But another did not come before it all would change.

Soon

There is another who watches the woods burn. She is new to these woods, but she is not new to Fairendale, though none of the people, as they are today, would recognize her. She has known this land since the day she was born, but she has come here a stranger. She stands at the edge of the woods, almost to its burning, and one would not be able to see her all that well if one were to look, for she is clothed in smoke and mist, though she wears the most beautiful dress of green silk that the kingdom has ever seen. Her hair is piled on her head, red and long and shining, and her eyes are of the deepest green, greener, even, than the leaves of the forest that, just now, are shriveling up in the heat of fire.

If one were to see her clearly, one might call her beautiful indeed.

She moves inside this corner of the woods, a corner that

does not dare burn with the presence of this powerful enchantress. She holds her staff toward the farthest side, and a house appears, a house that is not wide but is tall, leaning, and boasts a beautiful garden in the middle of flames. She must be very powerful indeed, to make a paradise such as this one. She moves through the gardens, opening flowers, tilting her head. She makes another flower bush, over beside the front entrance of her house, and she calls up some roses by the porch, and then she walks up the steps and into the house, where she outfits the walls and the two bedrooms and the kitchen and the den. There will be another one coming here, but not for some time. She must be patient. She will wait.

This enchantress, one might agree, is a master of magic, and her corner of the woods remains bright and green and full of color. She is a master of magic, and her house remains invisible to all except her and the few she will permit to see it.

But, mysteriously, the green corner of earth is not invisible at all, and if one were to walk through the woods as they will appear tomorrow, with their blackened trees grieving for all the men lost in the flames of the dragons, one would marvel at how this small patch of land was left completely untouched, how trees and bushes and flowers remained even while all the trees and bushes and flowers around them disappeared in a great roar of fire.

When our enchantress has done making her house and giving it just the right touches, she nods her head, as if there is another here with her already, and then she retires to her bed, for she is weary, and magic drains even one as powerful as she.

So she sleeps until the morning sky is late and full of sun, and the sun breaks holes through all the charred trees and reaches into her window. The smoke is still thick, but it does not congregate around her patch of land, and she looks out the window to see that the fire has ceased burning.

It is almost time. Oh, yes. It is almost time.

Still, she must wait. Someone is coming. She will find her, and then the events that have been ordained since Fairendale's earliest days will begin in earnest.

Prince Virgil wakes to the smell of smoke and the castle buzzing all around him.

Though the castle is far removed from the bounds of the forest, its people have watched the forest burning all night. Dragons, the servants say. Dragons are coming, and the servants flit about the castle with so much fear in their eyes that Prince Virgil knows he must find his father and discover how much truth is held in their words.

It is telling, dear reader, that the first person our dear Prince Virgil thinks to find is his father, in a confusing time such as this one. Prince Virgil, you see, has been sitting on that magical throne more and more of late, and he is beginning, alas, to forget all the light. There is still some left, yes. There is still some that his mother tends every night when she comes in to kiss her boy goodnight, but it is not much anymore. Sadly, the darkness has begun to win in our prince. So this is why, you see, he searches for his father rather than his mother.

But his mother is waiting in the halls between the throne room and her boy's room. Perhaps she has known, with the mysterious knowing that only a mother possesses, that her boy will wake wanting answers. And perhaps she wants to be the one to answer them, rather than allow her son to hear what answers his father may provide.

Queen Clarion catches Prince Virgil in her arms. He does not sink so easily into them anymore, for Prince Virgil is growing taller and harder. She kisses the top of his head, trying not to think that the reason he fights against her arms is because the darkness has already won. No, it cannot be. Her boy is still mostly good. Love holds him in the light, and this moment Prince Virgil surrenders.

"My dear boy," Queen Clarion says, until, finally, Prince Virgil pulls away to look in his mother's eyes. They are as beautiful as ever. Blue pools of kindness. He could get lost in the waters, but he notices a shadow at the corners. Sadness? Regret? It is impossible to read.

"What is it, Mother?" Prince Virgil says. A bit of him shakes, deep down. Perhaps he is aware of the battle waging over his heart.

She pulls him into one of the many chairs situated within the hallways of the castle. The hallways are long and taxing on servants who are sent from one end of them to the other all day. That is the accepted reason for the chairs. But most of those in the castle know that these chairs exist for King Willis, for he cannot traverse an entire hallway without growing weary. So the chairs are large and roomy.

Queen Clarion kneels before her son. "Something has happened," she says.

"Yes," Prince Virgil says. He had known it when he woke. The castle was never as loud as it is today.

"The woods are burning," Queen Clarion says. "They began burning last eve."

"Why?" Prince Virgil says. "Why are the woods burning?"

Queen Clarion looks at her son. She grips his hand. "They are saying it is because of the dragons."

Prince Virgil feels his legs grow cold. Dragons. He has never seen a dragon in all his years, but he has heard all the stories.

The dragons have never been friends of his family. What do the dragons want?

"Why would they burn the woods?" Prince Virgil says.

Queen Clarion shakes her head, her golden hair shifting across her shoulders. "We do not know. We wait for word."

"Is it my father's men?" Prince Virgil says.

"It is only speculation," Queen Clarion says. "But it is rumored that all your father's men have vanished."

"Killed by the dragons?" Prince Virgil says.

"Perhaps," Queen Clarion says. "Or perhaps by some other danger."

"What other dangers?" Prince Virgil says. "What other danger could set the forest on fire?"

Queen Clarion watches her boy, though she says nothing. She is looking for a trace of the goodness that used to shine from his face. Even his skin has begun to look older, wiser, perhaps. But his eyes. Yes. There is still kindness in his eyes. He is thinking, even now, of his friends, said to be in the forest.

"We have heard no word of the missing children," Queen Clarion says.

Prince Virgil nods but does not say any more.

"Virgil," his mother says. He looks at her. His brown eyes lock with her blue, and they are connected for one moment, two, three. He feels a warmth spread through his chest, and he does not want his mother to look away, ever. He only wants to feel the safety of her gaze upon him at all times, for this is security. This is love.

"If there are dragons, Mother," Prince Virgil says, for what he has read in his mother's eyes has given him great courage to speak his mind. "Will we not be destroyed?"

Queen Clarion drops her eyes then, staring instead at her hand covering Prince Virgil's. "It is uncertain," she says. She looks back up, fixes him with her warmth. "But we can hope for mercy."

"If my father's men crossed the boundary line, there will be no mercy," Prince Virgil says. He feels the icy dread begin to cool his mother's warmth.

"We do not know for certain," Queen Clarion says. "The dragons and the people have long been separated. Perhaps there is hope."

"The woods are on fire, Mother," Prince Virgil says. He stands now, his hands spread out beside him, as if he is asking a question with arms instead of his mouth. "What could there possibly be of hope when the woods burn?"

Queen Clarion, alas, cannot answer this question, for it has haunted her long into the night, from the first moment she saw the flickering light begin to the west of the castle and wondered what it meant. But she can do something more. She can weave a story. Stories always brings unexpected hope.

So she says, "Sit, my son. I would like to tell you something."

And Prince Virgil does. He is not so far gone that he cannot do as his mother asks.

Queen Clarion tells him the story that many of the village children have heard all their lives, but this boy has not heard since he was quite young. It is a story about dragons, about people riding the dragons, about provisions being obtained on the backs of dragons rather than the dangerous trips across the Violet Sea. She tells him of the partnership, of the love, of the kindness extended from man and dragon alike. She tells him how this partnership changed at the hands of King Sebastien, for the dragons had defended King Brendon, and King Sebastien could not forgive them for that. The dragons, in the war, lost many of their own, and they could not forgive that, either. And so both people and dragons lost much, but it was, perhaps, the dragons who lost the most, for they lost their very reason for loving the people. And the loss of love is a great loss indeed.

"So you see, my son, we used to have peace between us and the dragons," Queen Clarion says.

"That matters not now," he says. "There is no peace now." He motions toward the direction of the forest, though there are no windows where he and his mother sit.

"No," Queen Clarion says. She looks off toward the forest as well, hardly seeing the wall between her and the fire. "There is no peace now. But perhaps there might be." She touches her son's hand again. Her eyes grow wide. She smiles. "It is entirely up to you."

Prince Virgil does not say anything for some time. He is thinking over all that his mother has told him. Her story would make his grandfather solely responsible for the tension between people and the dragons, and his grandfather is dead. Her story would mean that though the dragons did not like the royal family when King Sebastien was on the throne, they loved the people still. It would mean that the dragons could be won again.

"Will they attack us before we might agree to peace?" Prince Virgil says.

"One cannot say for sure," Queen Clarion says. She eyes her son. "We are all in danger if they do. And if your father's men broke the treaty…"

"Why would they break the treaty?" Prince Virgil says. "Why would they go where they know they cannot go?"

Queen Clarion folds her hands across each other. "Your father is a difficult man to refuse," Queen Clarion says.

"They must have seen the missing ones," Prince Virgil says, and just like that, his eyes grow dark once more. Queen Clarion searches, but she cannot find the tiny spark that spoke of goodness. It has been swallowed by all the black. He continues on. "The missing ones must have crossed first. That is the only reason my father's men would have crossed as well."

"We do not know," Queen Clarion says, but her words are lost on her boy.

"I hope they were all consumed," Prince Virgil says. "I hope we never hear of them again."

"You do not wish it so," Queen Clarion says. "You speak before your heart is ready."

Prince Virgil narrows his eyes. He is not interested in hearing what his mother has to say. "I must go to my father," he says.

Queen Clarion places her hand on her son's arm. It is soft and gentle and warm, but he shakes it off all the same. He does not think kindly about the children who have crossed, whether there are friends among them. They are all foes to him now.

"Stay with me," Queen Clarion says. "Let us breakfast together."

Prince Virgil turns away. "Father is waiting."

Queen Clarion tries once more. "What if?" she says. "What if your friends died among the flames?"

The words hang between the two of them, daring Prince Virgil to choose, once more, mercy and compassion and goodness. And the battle thickens. If one were to look in Prince Virgil's eyes, one would see it quite clearly. There is the goodness, in light brown flecks. There is the evil, turning them black. Brown, black, brown, black, until, in the end, the black comes and stays.

"I do not care," Prince Virgil says. "The better that they die."

"No," Queen Clarion says, for she knows what his words mean.

"I hope they are gone," Prince Virgil says, his voice loud and authoritative, filling the entire expanse of the hall.

"No," Queen Clarion says once more.

"They do not deserve to live," Prince Virgil says. "They defied the orders of the true king." He spins on his heel and heads for his father's throne room.

"Virgil, please," Queen Clarion says. A mother cannot give up, you see.

He turns back. They are too far apart, but she crosses the distance with a swishing of skirts. She touches his face. "You are becoming a man," she says. His eyes soften again.

"So my father says," Prince Virgil says.

"You must choose to become a good man," she says.

"I am already a good man," Prince Virgil says.

"Yes," Queen Clarion says. "But sometimes we can lose who we are in the decisions we make." She bends her head closer, for Prince Virgil is not as tall as Queen Clarion yet. "Sometimes we can lose who we are in the decisions others make for us. Do not let that happen."

And it is with great triumph that Queen Clarion watches the flecks of goodness return to her son's eyes, for this moment at least.

"I shall not," Prince Virgil says.

"Beware of the throne," Queen Clarion says.

"My father…" Prince Virgil does not continue, but Queen Clarion knows that he is trying to tell her his father requires him to sit the throne at every session. She knows this. She has stared from the shadows when no one else was looking.

"Find me when you are done with your father," Queen Clarion says, for if she can undo the work of the throne, goodness might yet win for good.

Prince Virgil nods. He looks at her one moment more, and then he stalks away.

Queen Clarion watches him go, this son she has loved since the day he was born. He walks as she remembers his uncle walking. This gives her hope.

But a knot of fear makes its way into a corner of her heart, where it gazes around the warm chambers, burrows in so it is perfectly comfortable, and reaches its cold fingers out as far as it dares go.

Queen Clarion walks back to her chambers, where eyes do

not follow her every move, and weeps.

Prince Virgil does not go to the throne room, as his mother suspects. He ventures down into the dungeons beneath the dungeons, where he has never been before. He climbs down every twirling step along the staircase into the darkest dark he has ever known, with only a small candle to guide him, and all the while, his legs shake with a fear so thick he could reach out and touch it. He knows that the magical children are kept behind bars, as are all the prophets. He has no need to fear the people who are behind the bars. There is no magic in this dungeon. That was seen to long ago, when a skilled magician was said to have charmed the walls with a spell so strong it could never be undone. It was said that the spell not only kept prisoners inside their cells but it also stripped them of all magical ability. No one knows if this is so, for these dungeons had never been used until now, as far as anyone knows. But if one were to look, one might notice, in the corner of the darkness, far removed from the children and the prophets and the cell in which they have been kept, a pile of bones.

To whom do these bones belong? Well that, dear reader, is something we cannot say for now.

So as Prince Virgil descends these steps into the dungeons beneath the dungeons, he believes he is safe, but still fear grips him. For the darkness, what lives in our imaginations when darkness covers us, is another thing altogether.

Every now and again, Prince Virgil hesitates on the stairs, the candle shaking in his hands. Does he really want to do this? Does he really want to see starving children and prophets who have not known the sun for many days, and some of them years, and the woman with hair like serpents?

Something moves him again. Something pulls him down, down, down into the ground.

He hears the whimpering before he sees them. He has not yet rounded the corner that opens into the cell room. He is startled by his shadow on the wall, and then he smiles a bit to himself. It will be a fearsome sight for all the children. Well, good. They deserve a little fear for what they have all put the kingdom through.

When he rounds the corner, he scans the cell. There are bodies everywhere, lying on their backs, curled up on their sides, slumped along the walls, half dead it seems. Children are not nearly as populous as the old ones. Only the children and a handful of the prophets have lifted their heads to see who comes down the stairs.

"The prince," one of the prophets says. "The prince has

come to see us. How very kind." It is the old woman, half blind, for old eyes do not adjust quickly to light when they have spent so many days in dark. She must know his shape. Or perhaps she has seen him coming with her Sight.

The children sit up now. "Are we free?" one of them says.

Prince Virgil says nothing, though he has the sudden urge to laugh. What is wrong with him? He did not used to be so cruel. His vision grows blurry.

"Do you come to set us free?" another of the children says.

Prince Virgil shakes his head. "I cannot set you free," he says. "My father…" But he does not finish, and in the space between his words and whoever would speak next, Prince Virgil grows angry. It is not so easy describing this anger. He feels it begin in his heart and then move its scorching tide out through his fingers and, finally, his mouth. "You will never be set free." His voice is harder, deeper than he remembers, rough and ugly. The children gasp. One of them starts crying, and he likes the power their weakness has granted him. So he says the words again. "You will never be free."

"But we are innocent," a boy calls from the back. "None of us has a single bit of magic. They have tried us, and we cannot do it."

"But you could be lying," Prince Virgil says. "Or hiding your powers, as the boy in the kingdom did for many years."

"These children do not hide anything," says the prophetess Aleen. "The one you seek is out there." She points behind him. Prince Virgil has no way to guess in which direction she points, for the stairs and their twisting and turning and the blackness that surrounds their every side has eliminated all sense of direction Prince Virgil may have possessed, which, in truth, is not much.

But a curious feeling spreads through him now. He is glad, so glad, that his friend lives. And yet he is afraid. Need he fear Theo? Or has Theo fled forever?

"It is not easy to do the right thing when we see only what we want to see," Aleen says now. "These children." She motions behind her. "They are innocent."

"My father has a reason for their imprisonment," Prince Virgil says, though in this moment, he cannot quite remember what it is.

"And, pray tell, what is it?" says another prophet. He has a long white beard and eyes that Prince Virgil cannot quite see in the dark, as if they are holes instead of living, moving things.

Prince Virgil searches his mind for the right words, but they do not come easily. And then, finally, they do. "The people hid the magic boy from us all this time," Prince Virgil says. "They must pay."

"The children must pay?" Aleen says, at the same time

another boy, with a voice of the same tone and resonance as Prince Virgil, says, "We did not know of a magic boy."

And what if they did not know of a magic boy? Does that change what his father had done? Does it make it more cruel, more unnecessary? Prince Virgil is lost in a cloud of doubt and confusion. He sets the candle on the stone floor. Its flame shifts and dances.

"Your father wants you to see what he wants you to see," Aleen says. "It is not always the truth." She stares at the flick of fire.

The old man reaches through one of the bars, as though to touch Prince Virgil. But the prince is not so foolish as to stand close enough to be touched, so the man's hands wave in the air instead. Prince Virgil can see his eyes now, however. They are liquid blue, like a sky that is submerged in water. He feels a jolt. They are Arthur's eyes, only much older, set into waves of wrinkles.

"Prince Virgil," the prophet says. "Please. Come closer."

But Prince Virgil remains where he is. "Do you think I am so foolish as that?" he says. "Do you think I do not know what you want of me? You will never get it."

"What is it I want from you?" the old man says. "What is it you think I desire?"

"My life," Prince Virgil says. "My life for all of yours."

"No, my boy," the old man says. "I have seen what is coming. I know of the danger you are in."

Prince Virgil shivers. Danger? What is it that is coming for him?

"Is it the dragons?" he says, but the words come out hardly a whisper.

The old man says nothing.

"Tell me, boy, what is it you want with us?" the prophetess says. She wraps her bony hand around the iron bars. Her knuckles appear as black marbles in the shifting darkness. "What is it we can do to be shown a bit of kindness?"

"But we have been shown kindness—" a child begins to say.

"Shush," the old man says, turning toward the child. No one else speaks.

"Tell me where Theo is," Prince Virgil says. "Tell me where I can find him, and all of this can end."

"We know he is not here," Aleen says. "That is all."

"But you can See the future," Prince Virgil says.

"We only See the future that wants to be Seen," Aleen says. "Theo's future is not a future that wants to be seen."

In truth, dear reader, Aleen has not been able to See the future since she arrived here. She has depended on the gifts of Yerin and a handful of the other prophets who are not too weak to See. But her Seeing has gone dark.

"You are prophets," Prince Virgil says. "You are supposed to know things."

"Not all things," the old man says. "At times, the future remains silent."

"You have not Seen Theo in any of your visions?" Prince Virgil says. He does not believe them, and he is growing angrier by the moment.

"It is not easy to concentrate on visions when we are so hungry," Aleen says. The bars cut her face into four distinct pieces. "Your father is not so generous to those of us in the dungeon."

"You are given bread and water every day," Prince Virgil says, though he is not entirely sure they are. He knows nothing of what happens in a place as dark as this one.

"Yes," the old man says. "We are."

"Is that not enough?" Prince Virgil says.

Would it be enough for our prince? He does not ask the question of himself.

The old man gestures behind him. "There are many of us," he says, "and very little bread and water."

"You are not good for much," Prince Virgil says. "Perhaps I should just let you die."

Aleen smiles, with those white teeth of hers. They seem to glow in the dark. "You have too much goodness to let us die," she says.

Prince Virgil feels the warmth grip his heart once more.

"Tell me why I should let you live," Prince Virgil says. "What are you good for?"

The old woman tilts her head. She is two heads shorter than the man, but the tilt makes it appear as though she has lost another inch of her height. "What else are we good for, indeed," she says. "We populate your father's secret dungeon. We seem to be doing a well enough job of that."

"And that is where you shall stay," Prince Virgil says. "Until we find the missing ones." He takes a step closer, but then remembers the old prophet's arms and steps back once more. "Or until you tell me where I might find Theo."

"Everywhere," the old woman says. She backs away from the bars and throws her hands in the air. Then she moves close again. "And nowhere."

Prince Virgil moves as if to strike her, but she pushes away from the bars. His hands slam against iron instead.

"Ah," the old woman says. She smiles, her black skin dancing in the candlelight like some kind of shadow. "So you do have a bit of your father in you."

Prince Virgil shrinks back. No. He is nothing like his father. He would never hit a person. He would never hurt them. He looks at his hands that, moments ago, reached out to strike this ancient prophetess. His memory flashes. He sees his father strike Queen Clarion. His stomach clenches. Who has he become? Who is his father making him be?

His hand throbs from where it hit the cold iron, but sometimes it takes a bit of pain to help a boy remember who he is. And the iron bars have reminded him quite clearly. Aleen knew this, you see. It is why she provoked the boy. It is why she is smiling even now.

This boy is beginning to remember who he is. This boy is beginning to weep. "I only want this to be over," he says. "I only want it finished."

"As do we all," says the old man, and this time his hand comes through the bars and rests on Prince Virgil's head. It is a gentle hand. One that speaks of love and kindness and care. "As do we all."

Prince Virgil does not know what it is about that touch, but it feels familiar, as if he has felt a touch like this one before, in his dreams. Or in another life. Or, perhaps, before he was born. Would that be possible?

"How can we finish it?" Prince Virgil says.

"We wait," the old woman says. "We wait until the time is right."

"And how long might that be?" Prince Virgil says.

"Some time," the old woman says. "Some time yet."

"And how will we know it is finished?" Prince Virgil says.

"Oh, we will know," the old man says. "There is much more yet to come. And you will need to be brave and strong and true, my dear boy. Do you think you can be brave and strong and true?"

Prince Virgil looks at the man, and though he does not know quite what the old man means, he agrees. "Yes," he says. "I will."

"Good boy," the man says. He takes his hand from the top of Prince Virgil's head. "And what else is it that brought you down these stairs?" For the prophet knows what is in the heart of the boy, the two sides warring. He knows that Prince Virgil has also come here to see if he is good like his uncle and can help the starving children and the old prophets.

Prince Virgil looks at them, at all the children whose eyes he can hardly see, even by the light of his candle. He looks at the prophets, most of them lying still on the floor. He looks at the old man and the old woman, who seem to be the leaders of those trapped in these dungeons, and he wonders if he can, in fact, choose goodness. Might he dare defy his father and bring them food and light and water? Might he risk being banished from the kingdom as his uncle was before him, simply to meet the needs of strangers? Might he do it?

He looks at them for a very long time. They stare back at

him.

No, he decides. No, he cannot. The throne is too important. He cannot live without it, and, besides, he is not his uncle. He could not survive alone in the lands. He had never spent a night outside the castle before.

He is not a strong man as his uncle was. He is not sixteen. He is merely twelve.

"You could," the old man says, as if he knows precisely what Prince Virgil is thinking. He says nothing more.

Prince Virgil bends to retrieve his candle, turns and flees up the stairs, taking the light with him. He hears the children begin to wail behind him, and this makes him run ever faster, to get far, far away from the sound of starving children and the sight of an old man and woman who will probably die, with all the rest, inside their black prison.

He tries his best to outrun them, but a boy can never outrun his own mind. For the shadows of what he has seen and known in his life, the tragedies he has witnessed with his own two eyes, will haunt him until he looks them straight in the face. Prince Virgil cannot run from them forever.

Though he will try.

"Hush, children," Yerin says to the ones who wail. "Hush, now, my dears. All will be well. Someone is coming to help us."

"When?" the children say, for they think that perhaps this means they will be released from their prison and see the light of day yet again.

"Soon," Yerin says. "But, for now, let us sleep."

It is true, dear reader, that someone is coming. It is also true that he comes soon. But soon means different things to different people, and so we must wait to see what soon means to an old man like Yerin.

Battle

It was not that the dragons could hear the army marching through the forest, which was only called The Wood at the time of this tale. It was that they could feel them. They could feel every step. Zorag was only a young dragon of forty-three, and he heard it long before the others.

"Someone is coming," he said. "A great number of them."

His parents looked at each other. They had not yet felt the tremors. And when they did, they repeated his words. "Someone is coming," they said.

"I will go straight to King Brendon," said Zorag's father, Erell, and he took off. Zorag and his mother waited and waited and waited, and finally they heard the wings of his father flapping overhead. The ground was still rumbling. Their dragon scout had confirmed their fears: someone was marching through the forest. And it was a great number of someones.

Zorag's father landed before the multitude of dragons. He let out a thundering roar that shook the land more deeply than the footsteps did. The land held still for a moment, as if all the soldiers marching through it had suddenly stopped. All the dragons turned toward Erell. "An invasion," Erell said. "We shall help the king keep the peace. You remain here until I send instructions." He lifted off toward the castle. The dragons stared after him.

His mother looked at Zorag with eyes that spoke of worry, though she did not say anything but, "You must stay here, my son." She dipped her head, her ears flickering a little, as they did when she was nervous. She lifted off into the sky. Zorag saw two others do the same.

And of course he would not stay here. Of course he would go help. Of course.

After all, he loved a king, too.

His mother was watching the sky when he flew over it, but his father was staring at the king. Zorag landed behind his mother, at the precise moment his father lifted into the sky, with a girl on his back. He had seen the girl before. She was the king's daughter.

But Zorag did not have time to think on this, for the next moment the three dragons burst into action, taking to the sky. They breathed fire wherever they went. The forest burst into flames.

It was all madness after that. Zorag watched dragons fall from the sky, and he drew further and further back, in line with the castle and then behind the castle, for he did not know what this helping had meant back when he resolved to, and he was, after all, still a very young dragon. He had never seen battle like this before.

The land stilled. The people waited, and Zorag with them. And then his father dropped from the sky. He did not rise from where he landed. Zorag watched, a heat pulsing over his body that had nothing to do with the fire within. His father was dying. His father was dying. His father. He was dying.

Zorag watched, as if he did not live in this world but was only an observer. He watched King Brendon kneel before his father. He watched the king weep. He watched the lifeblood drain from the wound in his father's neck.

And then someone shouted, and before them all stood the men who had done this. Too many of them remained. Zorag, even in his shock, could see that clearly. The man with an army yelled something. And then one of the village people rushed forward, and madness broke free again.

The old king did not stand when it was all over. A new king did. He called from the castle steps.

"You," he said. Zorag did not turn, until the king said, again,

"You, dragon," and he realized that the king was addressing him. He must have ventured out from his hiding place, though one might argue that a dragon cannot very well hide with a body so large. Zorag saw that he was only steps from his dead father. He had intended to say a goodbye, perhaps.

But he turned to the new king instead.

"You will take my message to your people," the new king said. He was young and handsome, with dark hair and eyes that did not miss anything. He strode over to Erell's body on the ground. "You to your places and I to mine," the new king said. He lifted Erell's head, and Zorag roared. The new king waited until Zorag was finished. "Or you shall end up like this dragon." The new king sliced right through the head of his father, and tossed it in Zorag's direction.

Zorag felt the hate burning within him. His throat began to glow.

"I have magic like the world has never seen," the new king said. "I will defeat you."

And because Zorag was a young dragon, because he did not know so much about magic, only what King Brendon had shown him when he was a prince, Zorag could not say a word in return.

"Now go," the new king said. "Tell your people what has happened here. Tell them that if they cross into my land, this shall be their fate." He pointed his sword toward Erell's body.

Zorag roared again. He lifted into the sky.

"Go away and never come back," the new king shouted. And this is precisely what Zorag did. He took the message to the dragons, what few were left. His mother, alas, was not among them. They never found her body.

The hatred in Zorag's heart grew dark and cold. He would never, ever love another human being as long as he lived.

Unexpected

Maude and the children hide out in the cave that lines the boundary between Morad and the Weeping Woods. They have had no courage to do what must be done—run into the burning forest (though one might agree, this would not be the greatest plan), run for their lives, run back toward the only home they have ever known—and they are, in truth, starving. There has been no water but for the water Maude saved in a jar from the last time Arthur foraged. They have been sharing it, tiny little sips, but they are all weak and tired, and Maude knows they must move out of this place soon. They cannot die in a cave. They must at least try to live. For Arthur.

She has searched the land from the mouth of the cave, trying to find Arthur. She knows, of course, that searching from the mouth of a cave is not really searching at all, but it is all she can do, for now. Hazel wakes up every morning crying for her father.

The girl's eyes, today, are red-rimmed and purple. Maude is too afraid to cry. She is afraid that if she does cry, it will somehow make his death all the more real. She saw the bodies, so many of them. She had wondered if one of them was Arthur, though she could tell that most of the broken ones upon the ground wore the armor of the king's guard. Now the bodies have disappeared.

A whole army destroyed by the fire of dragons. It is quite astounding and, I am sure you will agree, very, very sad. They will not be returning to their families after all, as they had once hoped. How very sad indeed. But where is it the bodies have gone? Could there yet be hope? It is impossible to say for sure.

The dragons have vanished as well. In all the fire and smoke and tears, Maude and the children did not see where they went. And this is also what stays their flight, what keeps them in the dark cave rather than breaking free and running. They do not want to see the dragons again. They do not want to be consumed, as the king's men had been. Now that the treaty has been broken, Maude does not know what to expect. The dragons might attack anywhere. The woods have stopped smoking, finally. Perhaps they can move to safety at the day's end, though the Weeping Woods have not ever been considered safe. But, perhaps, the fire has purified them.

Maude has not slept in all the hours since the dragon's

attack. She has watched the woods, waiting for them to cool enough so that she and children might have a hope of escaping the dangers that lie in wait at, it seems, every turn. Though one might argue that the king's men are no longer a threat, for they lay in the dirt and did not rise, and then they vanished. Would anyone see Maude and the children emerging from this boundary cave?

The children watch the woods with Maude.

"The fire is out," says a boy named Chester.

"Yes," says Maude. "We must move soon."

"But what will we find in the forest?" Hazel says. "Are there not greater dangers inside?"

It is precisely what Maude has been thinking over these past hours, as she watched the fire dim and the smoke begin to fade. "Yes," she says. "But it is no different than anywhere else. Danger is all around."

The children know she is right. They shiver.

"Perhaps we should sleep," Maude says. She pats her daughter's leg. "We shall need our strength for the flight."

So the children stretch out as they have grown accustomed to stretching out, feet touching heads, bodies packed tightly around one another. It is cold in this cave, and they need each other for warmth. At least the woods will hold some warmth from the fire, though it will hold little else. What Maude has not let herself consider is what she and the children will do for food. The woods, you see, have been burned. There is not much life left within. Or is there? One can never really know these things when one lives in a world of magic.

Maude misses Arthur more than ever. She was never a planner in the way of escape and hiding and staying alive in such a desperate way. It is true that when she lived in the village, she planned her family's meals and their chores and their magic lessons, even. But she has never planned how to stay hidden from a king who searches. Arthur is the man for that. And Arthur is no longer here.

But Maude closes her eyes and tries not to think about all the questions that wait to be answered. She tries not to think about the magic that will be needed to keep them safe, though the children are far too weak for magic now. She tries not to think about where they might stay and what they might eat and who might be waiting for them. But it is not easy. No. It is not at all easy. Still, she attempts, closing her eyes, only to watch the thousands of possible outcomes play across the strip of her mind. The children are caught. The children starve. The children are carried off by fairies.

She has just fallen into a light sleep when Hazel says, "Mother?" Maude startles back awake. "Is it time?"

Maude looks toward the sky. It has begun to darken. Maude

rises from her spot on the ground. "Yes," she says. "Yes, it is time."

The children shuffle to their feet and wait for her instructions. Ursula, the girl with raven-black hair, calls out, "But what shall we do once we get there?" Her voice is high and uncertain, and Maude is rather glad that she cannot see the girl's face. "The woods are dead. There is nothing left inside."

"And our magic is gone," says the tiny girl, Lina.

They all look to Maude for their answer, but it has never been Maude who has had all the answers. It has always been Arthur. It has always been his job to figure out what to do next, and she has merely corrected his course a time or two, when she was fairly certain that he had it all wrong. And now it is up to her to figure out what to do, and she does not feel quite cut out for the task.

But she must. There are too many lives at stake.

"We shall figure something out," Maude says, trying to reassure the children with a confidence she does not feel herself. "As we always do." Hazel nods. She trusts her mother completely, you see. After all, her mother has always cared for her. Why would she stop now, even if her father is gone? She is terribly sad about her father being gone, but the other children have lost both their parents. She tries to think of them, but thinking of others who have lost the ones they love only widens the hole in her heart. She only hopes that she will be able to see her father again. Hazel only hopes she will be able to tell him how much she loves him, in case he did not know before. She only hopes that she will once again feel his arms around her, when they are reunited.

She does not know that her mother is hoping, right this minute, for the very same things.

"We shall find a place to live inside the woods," Maude says. "For a time. And then, when we are stronger, we shall make our journey to Rosehaven, as Arthur wished."

"Without father?" Hazel says.

Maude nods. Her eyes are dry, though she feels quite sad indeed. "Yes. Without your father. He knows where we are going."

"And Theo," Hazel says.

Maude's eyes soften. "Yes," she says, for she, too, feels the great chasm that lies before them. Half their family has been lost. But she does not have time to dwell on those losses as yet. They will keep her from moving forward, and if she and the children are to survive, they must keep moving forward.

She beckons to the children. "Follow closely behind me," she says. "We will return to the woods. Do not stop until I do."

What Maude does not say to the children is that they are far too weak to travel on a journey as far as Rosehaven. She does not tell them that it will take quite some time to gather enough strength from what they may find to eat in the charred remains of the woods. She does not tell them that they will, in fact, be hiding, once more, in the woods for, perhaps, longer than they expect, for she knows that all of these disappointments would end in only one possibility: The children would run. And in their running, they would scatter. And in their scattering, they would die.

And so she does what all mothers do at one time or another: she puts on a brave face and beckons them to follow her, though she knows that either way they go they might meet Death. "We will start over," Maude says, just before she moves from the cave.

Soon, they will have run all the way to the middle of the woods, nearly all the way to the other side. They will run until an unexpected sight will cause them to falter in their steps and stop.

If one were to look in between the trees that have, miraculously, even now, begun to green up again, one might see a figure limping through the forest, much ahead of the children, so he does not see them and they do not see him. He is a figure clad in dented iron, still shining where all the others were burned and blackened. He is on his way back to the castle.

Yes, dear reader. It is as you hoped. It is our good captain, Sir Greyson.

Our hero has survived a battle with the dragons, and now he is on his way to tell the king what has happened. Or perhaps he will stop in to see his mother first. There is no way to know which he will choose, for both possibilities battle in his head, and this part of the forest lies at the edge of the village. He must walk through it to get to his king.

He walks right past the house of the Enchantress, but he is too torn with grief to notice, too regretful of his order to those brave men who still lie, slain—burned, really—on a battlefield, too angry at the king who was the cause of it all. If the king had not told them to find the children at all costs, Sir Greyson never would have put his men in danger. They would never have died such useless deaths. What was the point of it, after all? They did not have the children. They only had death.

Death has not been kind. It has left no man standing. No man but he, that is, for he was so far behind his men that when his horse saw the destruction of fire, he threw the captain off his back, and Sir Greyson turned on his heel and fled.

And now he is left to deliver the news to the castle. He does not want to deliver it to the soldiers' wives. Oh, no. They have lost so much already.

But let us see what this good man does. He walks from the woods. He stops at a house. He puts his hand on a door. He waits. Should he go in? Should he continue on?

He enters.

His mother is lying on a bed. She raises herself when he comes in. "My son," she says, for she knows him immediately, though he wears his helmet. This is the way mothers know their sons, you see.

"Mother," he says, and he falls into her arms. He weeps as he has never wept before, though his face plate keeps all but the sound of his weeping from his mother.

"Oh, child," his mother says, though he is no longer a child. Perhaps men are always children to their mothers. "What is it?"

"My men, Mother," he says. "All of them are gone."

"Gone, my son?" his mother says. "Whatever could you mean?" for this woman does not know the news of the kingdom without her son. She only knows that her son has not come for several days, has not delivered her medicine, which ran out the first day Sir Greyson and his men entered the woods, and she can feel the sickness spreading into her legs. She is glad he is here now. He can give her the medicine that will stave off her pain, and she might rise from her bed again.

"My men," he says. "Burned up by dragons." His eyes fill with tears once more. He has removed his helmet, so his mother is witness to his pain. His mother pats his back, trying not to cry, too. She is a compassionate woman, you see. She cannot bear to see her boy cry, for it tears at something in her heart, too. She is a mother who wants to make it better, but there is no way of making a tragedy such as this one better. She does not ask questions. She merely listens. She merely holds him and waits.

"The king," her son says. "The king wanted so badly to find the missing children. And we did. They were with the dragons."

She puts the pieces together, for she is a wise woman. She knows that the children must have been with the dragons and her son's men must have crossed the border and then all madness must have broken loose, as it would with a treaty broken and dangerous dragons. She had never trusted the dragons, even back when the people of Fairendale used them for their travels. They were too powerful, she always thought. She mistrusted their intentions.

"And what of the children?" Sir Greyson's mother says.

Sir Greyson shakes his head. "I do not know what became of them," he says. "They might be dead."

"Perhaps you should tell the king all this," his mother says.

"I was on my way," Sir Greyson says. "But I have not seen you in so long." He pulls away from his mother now. He peers into her face. "I have been gone for some time. You need your medicine."

"Yes," his mother says. Her eyes laugh a little. "Yes, I do."

He pulls a vial of medicine from his pocket and shakes it rhythmically, drops it into the space inside a needle and then inserts the needle into his mother's leg. "I am sorry, Mother," he says.

"For what, my son?" she says.

"For neglecting you," he says. "I got here as quickly as I could."

"I know you did," she says.

Sir Greyson bends over her and kisses her forehead. "I shall return soon," he says.

She watches him go, knowing it may be quite some time before she sees him again. The king is not a gracious man, and when her son tells him this story, he could very well imprison Sir Greyson or send him away without honors. There is no way of knowing what it is the king might do.

She will soon be gone. And then her son can make a life of his own, instead of working for a man as cruel as King Willis and doing what he knows to be wrong. She only hopes that she will not leave this world too late.

Sir Greyson walks up the path with a slow step, a bent over

back and the weight of death on his shoulders. He passes the mermaids who call to him and knocks on the large oak door of the castle with the brass bear placed there for such a purpose. A servant opens the door. His mouth drops open, as if he is surprised to see a soldier standing at the door. He opens it wider, and Sir Greyson steps inside.

"I will let the king know you are here, sir," the servant says and scuttles off toward the king's throne room. Sir Greyson takes his time, trying to figure out just how much he is going to say. If he indicates that all the children are dead, perhaps he will be released to return home to his mother. But that would be defying his honor, for, of course, he does not know for sure whether they are dead or alive. He only knows that he saw dragons, that all of his men are dead and that the children disappeared. For all he knows the dragons might have taken them back to a hiding place where they shall remain safe for all the rest of the king's days.

Hope flutters in his chest.

So what is it that he will tell the king?

Well, he has no more time, for the throne room doors are opened at this very moment, and he steps onto the red carpet, with only the distance between the doors and the throne to find his words.

The king waits until Sir Greyson is halfway into the room to speak. "So," he says. "So you have come back to us. This is quite unexpected."

"Yes, Sire," Sir Greyson says. He is still walking. He notices that the king's son is standing just beside the throne. The prince's hair and face seem darker than Sir Greyson remembers. Darker enough to look at the prince twice, in quick succession, as if it is a completely different boy who stands before him as a prince. But no. The face is the same. Only more sinister. Sir Greyson swallows hard. He had hoped that Prince Virgil might break the reign of evil in Fairendale. But seeing that boy, seeing the change, has told him otherwise.

He hopes all the harder that the children live still.

"Tell me," the king says. "Tell me what you know of the children."

Sir Greyson feels the contempt for his king strike him hard and fast between the shoulders. King Willis, you see, did not even ask about the welfare of Sir Greyson's men. A king who cares not for how many soldiers gave their lives so they might carry out his commands. A king who thinks only of himself and a throne and securing it for generations to come. What does a kingdom do with a king like this one?

If Sir Greyson carried dislike for his king before, it turns, quite rapidly, to hate, though Sir Greyson has never been able to hold hate as others might.

Prince Virgil tilts his head and narrows his eyes, as if he can see what lies behind the look on Sir Greyson's face. And perhaps he can. Sir Greyson was never one for hiding what he felt. Which is precisely why he wears a helmet in the presence of the king. But, if you remember, Sir Greyson removed his helmet at his mother's house. It is, unfortunately, still there, on the table beside her bed.

Sir Greyson takes a deep breath. "I know not what happened to the children," he says. He tries quite hard to keep the contempt from burdening his words.

The king roars, his eyes turning from curious to angry in only a matter of seconds. "What do you mean you do not know? How could you not know what happened to the children when you had them in your hands?"

"With all due respect, sire," Sir Greyson says. "We did not have them in our hands. We followed them to the dragon lands, but we did not touch them."

"Did not touch them," King Willis says. "Tell me, what is the difference? You had them within your sight, did you not?"

"Yes, sire," Sir Greyson says.

"And what is the difference between seeing them and seizing them, when you are hundreds and they are only a few?" King Willis says. He is pacing the platform where his throne sits.

It does not take the most brilliant of minds to know that

seeing children in the middle of Morad and seizing children in the middle of Morad are two very different things, with many, many steps between. But Sir Greyson merely humors his king. "They stood with dragons, sire," he says. "I did not want to place my men in danger."

"And yet your men died," King Willis says. His eyes turn upon Sir Greyson, with darkness that cannot be contained. "They died, and you have nothing to show for their sacrifice."

Sir Greyson feels the sadness brimming toward his mouth. He swallows it down and blinks hard. "Yes, sire," he says. His voice is thick. He does not say more. He does not need to say more.

"The dragons," King Willis says now, satisfied that his words of attack have hit their mark. "They defied their treaty." He folds his hands together and brings them to his lips. When he takes them away, he says. "What shall we do about that?"

Sir Greyson shakes his head. "No, sire," he says. "They did not defy their treaty."

"They did not?" King Willis says, this time surprised by what Sir Greyson has to say. "Then, tell me, what happened?"

"One of my men," Sir Greyson says, but he cannot finish, for he can only see their bodies, lying on the ground he fled. "I am sorry," he says, but it is too soft for Prince Virgil or King Willis to hear.

"What is it you say?" King Willis says.

Sir Greyson clears his throat. "One of my men crossed the border. He tried to take the children. The rest of my men followed in the confusion. The dragons were only defending their own territory."

"So we defied the treaty," King Willis says, and, for the first time since Sir Greyson entered the room, King Willis looks frightened. "That means…" But he does not finish now.

Sir Greyson is not thinking of what it means. He is only thinking of his men. "I lost them all," he says. "Every one of my men."

King Willis looks toward his captain of the king's guard. "You lost every man?"

"Yes, sire," Sir Greyson says.

"No man but you lives?" King Willis says, as if this is too unbelievable for even a man like him.

"No man," Sir Greyson says.

"And how many men was it you lost?" King Willis says.

"Two hundred nine, sire," Sir Greyson says. He chokes on the number. It is a number far too great for him. It is a number far too great for Death and sorrow and loss and one man.

"You must prepare more men," King Willis says. "The dragons will come. They will want war. We must be ready."

"But I have no more men," Sir Greyson says. "I have used

every man this kingdom had."

"You will gather more," King Willis says. "Lincastle is a good place to start."

"But sire," Sir Greyson says, but the king holds up a hand.

"You will gather more," King Willis says. "You will leave immediately."

Poor Sir Greyson. He has only just seen his mother, after many long days of leaving her to her sickness. What will he tell her now?

The thought of his mother makes Sir Greyson brave. "Might I ask for a bit of leave, sire?" Sir Greyson says. He does not say more, though the look on his face says there is much more. Perhaps we might surmise what it is on his mind. Perhaps he would like leave to care for his mother. Perhaps he would like leave for the exhaustion that buckles his knees even now, clanking them against the armor that is the only reason he remains standing. Perhaps he would like leave because he was the only one of two hundred nine men who survived the fire of the dragons.

The king releases a long, bellowing laugh. "You are in jest, my good man," he says. "Leave at a time such as this."

Sir Greyson merely stares at him, for he was not, in fact, jesting. He does not say more, though, for he knows there is no arguing with a king like this one. He will have to prepare, alone, for immediate departure. His eyes feel heavy just thinking of it. Lincastle is a week's journey at least, more when one is as indisposed and weary as Sir Greyson.

Perhaps he could desert. Perhaps he could take his mother with him and be gone from this land, far away from where the king might find him. Perhaps he could take her to Guardia, or to the wastelands of Ashvale. Surely it was habitable now. It has been many years since the last fire mountain exploded.

No. Of course he cannot desert. He is a man of honor, after all. And where might he get his mother's medicine, if not from the king?

Sir Greyon risks one more plea. "Please, sire, allow me to tend my mother before I go," he says. He watches the prince look at the king. The prince's eyes are soft, now the color of the dirt in the village garden, rather than a midnight sky. Is that compassion we see? Why, yes, dear reader. It is.

But the king roars. He is angry. He is annoyed. He has had absolutely enough. "There is not a moment to lose," he says. "You shall go now."

The throne room doors fling open, as if they were waiting for this dismissal all along. Sir Greyson turns toward them, takes one step, two, and falls to his knees.

"Father," he hears the prince say.

"Get up," the king says.

"Father, he is not well," the prince says.

"Get up!" the king roars. And Sir Greyson tries, he does, but it is all too much—the despair, the weariness, the hopelessness of it all. The prince moves to his side and wraps his arms around the captain's armored belly. He pulls Sir Greyson to his feet. Sir Greyson turns to thank the boy, and the eyes startle him, more like wet earth with tiny flecks of gold in them. Prince Virgil nods at Sir Greyson. The prince's eyes fill, and he turns away.

And this, one small little gesture by a boy, gives Sir Greyson a strength that rises up within him and pulls him out the doors. It is only when he stumbles through the entrance of the castle that he looks down at his hand to see what is held within it.

A vial. Medicine.

His mother will not die while he is away.

Dear, sweet Prince Virgil.

Sir Greyson squeezes the vial in his hand and somehow, in spite of his faltering knees, runs back to the village.

Father

They lost many in the Great Battle. Many of them were elder dragons, who knew how to properly lead the dragons in the land of Morad. Many of the dragon families were left with only one mate to raise their children, or none at all.

There was a dragon, a very young one of only twenty-one years, just a baby, really, who had lost both father and mother in the Great Battle. His mother had been sister to Zorag's mother, and Zorag knew that he would have to raise him as his own, though he himself was young as well.

The young dragon, Blindell, was known to be an impetuous one, who preferred danger over safety. Zorag had seen Blindell cross into the woods, even, and had warned him multiple times in the last few days alone to stay far away from the land of Fairendale. He would risk the lives of all the dragons.

But Blindell had simply said, "They could never kill me," as if he, alone, were impenetrable. And it is true that he was a Fury, that he was a revered dragon among the dragons, for Furies were known to spike men faster than men could draw a sword. But he was a young dragon. He had not been trained in fighting, for the land of Morad was, until the new king marched on it, a peaceful land.

Blindell showed a fierce madness already, as if he were a dragon bred for battle. His father had been a foreigner to the lands of Morad, come from a distant land that might have been savage. Zorag's uncle had not spoken much of his homeland. They did not know anything about him at all. And now he had left his son, reckless and powerful. Truth be told, Zorag was a bit afraid of the young dragon, though he tried his best not to show it.

In the days after the Great Battle, Zorag stayed away from his cousin, too wrapped up in his own grief to notice the grief of others, though he was now the leader of the land.

And then, one day, Zorag spoke to Blindell, for he felt the time had come.

"Blindell," he said. His cousin's eyes found his. They were red, with flecks of brown and black in them. They were the kind of eyes meant to scare a man.

"Cousin," Blindell said.

"Come," Zorag said. "Fly with me." He took to the sky.

Blindell followed. Zorag led the way to a distant mountain. The two dragons landed together on the top.

"What is it, cousin?" Blindell said. "I know there is something. You have not spoken to me in all these days, except to warn me away from the boundary line." Blindell's eyes flashed and sparked.

"Yes," Zorag said. "I suppose I have been caught up in running Morad."

In truth, Zorag had not been caught up in running Morad, for he had been doing nothing at all. Grief, you see, takes time to fade.

"I suppose," Blindell said. He looked off in the distance, his eyes ever turned toward Fairendale.

"You need a father," Zorag said. "Yours died bravely, but it is time for you to take another."

"And who might that be?" Blindell said. His voice was a low rumble, as if he held back an anger that could consume him in a moment. "YOU?" His eyes narrowed, the black in them deepening.

"Yes," Zorag said quietly. "Me."

Blindell was silent for a moment, looking off toward the land and the forest and the faint outline of the castle. "They should have to pay for what they did," he said.

"We have promised peace," Zorag said. "And we shall keep

it."

"It is a coward's way," Blindell said.

"No," Zorag said. "It is brave to keep peace when so much has been lost."

"You are a fool," Blindell said.

Zorag growled. "Peace is what King Brendon would have wanted," he said. "He would not have wanted to risk the lives of the dragons."

"They killed our parents," Blindell said. "Does that not bother you?" Zorag did not say anything, so Blindell continued. "They damaged your wing. You cannot even fly properly anymore."

Zorag eyed his bent wing. He had not even known that he had carried this wound during the Great Battle. It was only when he returned to Morad with the new king's message that he felt its pain at all.

"It will heal in time," Zorag said.

Blindell let out a roar that shook the mountain. "It will not heal in time," he said. "Nothing will heal in time."

Zorag looked toward the castle, where he had seen the good king's fall. Where he had seen the new king slice through his father's head with hardly an effort. Where he had witnessed a magic stronger than any he had ever seen.

"The new king has magic," Zorag said, though this is, of

course, not the only reason he would not attack the kingdom.

"Magic is nothing to fire," Blindell said. "He does not deserve to live. I will torch their castle. Only say the word."

"Stone does not burn," Zorag said.

"But it breaks," Blindell said.

"Some of King Brendon's people are still there," Zorag said. Blindell did not answer. "You must rid yourself of your anger, cousin. Anger does not solve anything."

"Neither does peace," Blindell said.

They remained quiet for a very long time. And then, finally, Blindell said, "Yes. I will be your son."

Zorag dipped his head, though he felt much too young and ill-equipped to raise a son. But he would do what needed to be done. He would train Blindell. He would find the goodness in his cousin's heart. He would show him love.

And this, in the end, would save the entire dragon race.

House

Cora stands in the village streets, hidden in shadow. She considers what she must do. She watches the captain of the king's guard move through the streets in a flash that is uncharacteristic of this captain of the king's guard. She stands watch outside the window of the house into which he disappeared. She sees him measure the medicine. She sees him inject it into his mother's leg. She sees him place it in a cupboard, behind a stack of bowls. And after he leans down to kiss his mother's forehead, after he stands to watch her a moment longer, after he has slipped from the door of the cottage and off toward the castle, but not quite, she slips to the doorway. She turns the knob, for the houses in a village as peaceful as Fairendale have no locks to keep the world outside. She walks inside and moves toward the chair that sits beside the bed of Sir Greyson's mother. She takes the old woman's hand.

Why is Cora here? It is difficult to say. Perhaps she loved this woman once. Perhaps she loved this woman's son. One does many unexplainable things for love.

Cora remains in the chair all that evening and into the night. And when the first light of day appears in the east, she slips out and into her feathers. It is a blackbird that calls for the village people, just as Cora's plans had told them.

"It is time," the blackbird calls, and the people stream from their houses and follow the bird to the steps of the castle.

Prince Virgil is with his father in the throne room yet again. This time Queen Clarion is with them. They are talking about Sir Greyson and the king's men and all the children who still remain missing.

Queen Clarion watches her son, sitting beside his father on the throne, and it is with great sadness that she notices how he pays more and more attention to his father's manner of speaking and manner of doing and manner of being than he once did. What might she do to get her son back? She does not know that yesterday he slipped the captain of the king's guard a vial of medicine that would keep the captain's mother alive while he was gone on yet another journey. She does not know that the light has been warring with the dark relentlessly. She only sees which has won now, today. It is, sadly, the darkness once more.

She grieves this loss, as any mother would, for her son is a good boy. He truly is. But in the presence of his father, in the presence, she suspects, of that throne, her son becomes unrecognizable to her. Yet still she loves. Still she tries to grasp for the light and draw it out. This is why she is here, today.

His father has had too much influence of late.

"Do you think more men will come to fight our battles, Father?" Prince Virgil says. "Will they fight the dragons for us?"

"We do not know for sure whether we will fight dragons," King Willis says. "But the men of my father's homeland will come."

Queen Clarion is not so sure. King Sebastien was not a loved man, you see. He did not endear himself to the people of his homeland as King Willis seems to think.

"But what of the dragons, Father?" Prince Virgil says. "What if they should attack before the captain returns?"

"They are too afraid to attack," King Willis says, as if he has forgotten that his kingdom has no defense against any foe.

"But we have no king's guard," Prince Virgil says. "Anyone could attack. And we would not have protection."

"They do not know of this," King Willis says. "We lost our guard days ago. They have not attacked yet. There is a reason for that."

"And what of the children?" Prince Virgil says. "Where are they?"

Thinking of the children brings Prince Virgil back, momentarily, to the light, for love is a strong light. And Prince Virgil, whatever else he may have forgotten, has not forgotten the love he has for Theo and Hazel and Mercy. He has not forgotten that he wishes them, at least in this moment, safe and sound.

The throne seems to glow brighter. Prince Virgil's gaze is caught, and as quickly as he remembers his love, it is gone. There is only the throne and the kingdom and the rule he must have. He rests his head on the golden legs. They are cold and hard.

King Willis looks at his son. "And how would I know where the children are?" he says. "The captain did not say. They might very well be dead."

"But we do not know for sure," Queen Clarion says, for she hopes it is not true. She cares nothing for a throne, you see. She only wants her son to find happiness and love, and, yes, the goodness contained within him. "Perhaps they have escaped." Prince Virgil turns to her. His eyes are so black they make her shiver. She has never noticed how much he looks like his grandfather.

"They might have the help of the dragons," Prince Virgil says to his father.

"Perhaps," King Willis says. "But we will find them. You will see. We shall restore the kingdom, and your claim will be safe." King Willis pats his son's head. "You will be safe, my child."

"And when we find them, what will happen to the children?" Prince Virgil says. "What will we do with them?"

"Well," King Willis says. "They must die, of course."

Queen Clarion feels the words wrench open a cavern in her heart, for there was another man who spoke those very words once, when she was but a child. When she loved a boy who was banished forever. When the brother who remained asked his father what would happen if Wendell ever came back.

And Wendell had disappeared forever.

She watches her son's smile spread across his face, and she feels it snake across her own skin and deep into the pit of her stomach, where it turns thick and cold.

Perhaps he is already too far gone to be pulled back into the light. She had hoped it was not so.

As a mother always does.

The children and Maude have been searching for a good

place to hide all this time. All this time they have hidden in the forest, out in the open air, hoping that no one will be able to see them like they can see through all these burned-down trees, hoping that no one will venture inside the still-smoking forest. The trees, it is true, have begun to show green again, for this is an enchanted wood, after all, but they are not nearly so decorated as they were mere days ago. And without magic, Maude and the children are lost, it seems. Maude has begun to despair, for they have found no food or water or anything that speaks of life. They have wandered to nearly every corner of the woods, though there is one they have yet to find.

And this one, as it happens, is just the right one.

But we are getting ahead of ourselves. Let us first observe the children. They are tired and thirsty and hungry. But mostly thirsty, for a body, you see, cannot survive for long without water. And they have no Mercy to summon water from the ground. They have only staffs that do not work properly anymore, for children who starve are children with very weak magic.

They run still, looking about them at tree after tree after tree. They have seen them all, or so they think. The children weep. They do not weep noisily, for they do not want to upset Maude. They weep silently, holding hands behind their leader, who, though they cannot see it, weeps as well. Soon they will run out of tears, if they do not find water.

They stopped once to observe the astonishing sight of charred trees bearing green, so soon after a fire, and they stop now, as well, this time because they cannot continue on. Some of them place their hands on their knees and breathe in heaving gasps. Maude lifts her face to the sky and pants.

Hazel moves to her mother's side. She takes her mother's hand. She hopes that her presence might comfort Maude, but who can be comforted when they have lost a son and a husband? Maude certainly cannot. She has no plan, no focus, no hope, for grief has begun to steal the very life from her bones. Hazel cannot bear to see her mother walking as if she is nothing more than a sorcerer's apparition.

"We must keep moving, Mother," Hazel says.

"I cannot," Maude says. "I am too weak."

"We must, Mother," Hazel says. "We must, or we risk dying."

"I have already died a thousand deaths," Maude says, which is, perhaps, a poetic way of saying that grief can often steal our very lives. Maude is not usually so poetic. She is thinking of Arthur. It is something he told her long ago.

"Look at all of us, Mother," Hazel says. "Look how many look to you, Mother." And Maude does look, but it does not help to look at the children, for looking at the children only reminds her that she has lost her beloved Theo and her beloved Arthur, and this burden feels much too heavy for her shoulders. Hazel draws her mother to her feet. "We must go," she says.

Maude gazes at Hazel, and Hazel's eyes remain focused on her mother's face. And because Maude can see in her daughter's eyes a vestige of hope, it becomes a vestige of hope in Maude's heart as well. She takes a breath and turns to the children. "Come," she says. "We must move." But she is too weak to take a step.

Hazel puts her mother's arm around her, and one of the girls, the one called Ursula, moves to Maude's other side and stretches her arms around Maude's waist, though it does not take much stretching. Maude has grown painfully thinner in the days after the roundup. The two girls let Maude lean on them, and they begin to move forward again. The other children follow, no one saying a single word until another set of twins, these two born without the slightest hint of magic, say, at the same exact time, "Look," and all the children do. They do not see anything.

"It is a house," says one of the twins, Chester.

"Right there," Charles says.

The children look again. There is no house.

Have you ever heard of the boy who cried wolf, dear reader? The boy who cried wolf is a boy who went out to tend his sheep and, because he found it funny, would return to the village crying about a wolf trying to eat his sheep. He was never in any danger, but merely wanted to have a little fun. He did this three times, and each time the village people rushed to save the boy's sheep from a wolf that did not exist. And then, the fourth time, when the boy really was in danger, no one came to rescue him, for the people did not wish to be fooled again.

Chester and his twin brother, Charles, were known among the village children as pranksters. They have never, alas, heard the story of the boy who cried wolf, and so they could not be warned that a boy who initiates too many jokes is a boy who will not be taken seriously.

So it is that when they both say they see a house, and no one else sees it, the children do not believe them.

"Stop trying to fool us, Chester," Hazel says. "There is no house. There is nothing."

"But there is," Charles says. His face is completely serious, but this is a look the children have become quite familiar with over the weeks. This is a look both Charles and Chester wore when they told the story of how their parents descended from a long line of royalty, and it turned out not a bit of their story was true. This is the look they wore when they said they did not set spiders free in the house beneath the ground, though every child knew it was only Chester and Charles who would do such a thing. This is the look they wore one night at dinner, in the underground home, when they said that what they had before them was a hulking slab of roast lamb in a honey sauce, though the children only saw bread.

The children are familiar with these identical faces, and they will not fall for the antics of Chester and Charles once again. Children do not like their hopes dashed so violently as they are dashed when they find that something they hoped was true is, in fact, not true in the slightest. So the children ignore them.

"Hazel," Chester says, pulling on Hazel's ragged blue sleeve. "You do not see the beautiful trees?"

Hazel squints her eyes in the direction he is pointing. As far as she can see there are only burned trees with little bits of green to tell they are still alive. "No," she says. "I see only blackened trees."

"But they are green!" Charles says. He points to the same place Chester pointed. "A house and flowers and trees. How did they survive the fire? It must be magic."

The children shake their heads and follow Hazel and Ursula and Maude in the other direction. Chester and Charles take off toward the invisible house that no other children can see. Hazel looks back once, with a "We must stay together," and then does not look back again until she hears a voice that is most definitely not the voice of a boy or a child at all.

"Well," the voice says. "I see you have found me."

Hazel whirls around. Maude stumbles. And now there is a

house. There are trees. There are flowers, right in the middle of a burned forest. It is impossible and wonderful all at once. Where did it come from? How did it survive? Who is the woman before them? These are all the questions that fly through Hazel's mind as she follows the twins toward the house she can finally see.

The woman who stands outside the front door must be royalty, for she wears a flowing green dress trimmed in gold and jewels. It is full and wide and its collar reaches her chin. Her hair is kept back from her face, but Hazel can see it is red, like her lips. The woman's eyes flash green, and Hazel steps closer. The eyes are somehow familiar and unfamiliar all at the same time. Hazel feels a pain in her chest and drops her eyes to the gold necklace around the woman's neck. It is a blackbird.

Hazel speaks for Maude and the children. "We search for a safe place to hide," she says. She cannot keep her eyes from moving toward the house. A soft bed. A warm supper. Water. They need so much.

The woman stands with a straight back and a chin that tilts up and slightly sideways, as if she greets the world with curiosity. She is very beautiful.

"And your search has brought you here," the woman says. She has a smile that does not quite touch the sides of her eyes.

"Might you help us?" Hazel says.

Maude has come alive beside her. "My husband," she says.

The woman stares at Maude. "Your husband?"

"Does my husband live?" Maude says.

The woman moves her hands in front of her. "I cannot know such things," she says. She looks at Hazel. "But I might be of some help."

"Who are you?" Hazel says.

"I am called the Enchantress," the woman says.

"We need a place of refuge," Hazel says. "Perhaps a house that is like yours."

"Invisible," the Enchantress says. "To the ones who mean you harm."

"Yes," Hazel says. "Or perhaps invisible to everyone, if it can be done." She looks at the woman, who must have quite a gift of magic, for she lives in an invisible house. Hope begins move, warm and slow, from her heart to her throat.

"You have magic, do you not?" the Enchantress says. "Why not use your own?"

"The children are starving," Maude says now. She has straightened up beside Hazel and Ursula. "They cannot do magic when they are starving. We have not had enough water for days."

"So you will need food and water as well," the Enchantress says.

"Yes," Maude says. "If it might be arranged."

"I am quite skilled in the gift of magic," the Enchantress says. She nods her head in Maude's direction. "I can do all you ask and more, if you need it. But there is a price to be paid. Surely you know that."

"Yes," Maude says. "And what is your price?"

"I will do everything you have asked," the Enchantress says. "I will give you a house that is invisible to everyone who ventures inside these woods, if anyone is left. I will set up a garden that you and the children might tend. I will give you food and water, and you will eat as you have not eaten in many days." As she is speaking, the Enchantress looks at the children, each in turn. Then she looks back at Maude. "And I will take her."

She points to Hazel.

"Oh, no," Maude says. "No, no, no. Not my daughter."

The woman's hands turn up at the palms. She raises them at her side. "Then I am afraid I cannot help you." She turns.

"Wait," Hazel says. The Enchantress turns around again. Hazel looks at her mother. She puts her hands on Maude's cheeks. "Mother," she says. "Think of the children."

Maude's eyes are streaming. She does not try to wipe her tears away. They splash onto Hazel's small fingers. "I cannot think of the children, dear," she says. "I have lost everything. You are the only one left."

Ursula steps forward. "Take me instead," she says.

The woman shakes her head. "I am afraid that will not do," she says. Ursula frowns in her direction, but she steps back to Maude and Hazel.

"We will find Father and Theo," Hazel says. "I promise it. As soon as the danger is over."

"The danger will never be over," Maude says. Her voice has grown hysterical. "I cannot lose you, too. You are the only reason I am still running. You are the only reason I am still fighting."

Hazel shakes her head. "No, Mother," she says. "There is more than that. I know you." She gestures to the children, lined up in a wall-like fashion. "You are fighting for all of them. And you must keep fighting. You must agree to do as the Enchantress wishes. We must live."

Maude shakes her head. "No," she says. "No, I will not."

"You must, Mother," Hazel says. She brings her face close to her mother's. "For me. And Theo. It is what he would have wanted." And then she pulls her mother into a tight embrace. Hazel releases Maude and turns without another word. She nods at the Enchantress. "Very well," she says. "I will come with you as soon as you do as you have said."

"I have already begun it," the Enchantress says. She points to a spot, five hundred feet away, where a house grows from the earth in the shape of a shoe.

"A shoe?" Maude says in surprise.

The Enchantress smiles. "It will be a home," she says. "Take a look inside."

And so Maude and the children do. Hazel wishes more than anything that she might go inside, too, but she made a deal. So she turns to the Enchantress, who beckons her toward the front door of her much smaller house. "Come with me," she says. "I know just the place to put you."

"Wait," Hazel says. The Enchantress turns. "First I must know who you are." She stares at those green eyes that disturb her with their familiarity. Something about them comforts her, as if they belong to a friend. She does not remember meeting a beautiful woman like this one ever before in her life.

"I have already answered your question," the Enchantress says. "I am called the Enchantress. That is all you need to know." She moves toward the door, her skirts billowing out behind her. Hazel follows her inside.

Promise

There came an evening when Zorag felt the ground rumble in an altogether different way, as if only one walked where many had once come. It had been many years since the Great Battle. The other dragons did not seem to hear it, for they were still sleeping, but Zorag always had quite an extraordinary sense for these things. Even his mother, when she was alive, would comment on his ability to warn the dragons when any danger was near.

Zorag ventured to the edge of the Weeping Woods, which had found a new name after the new king invaded. It was appropriately named, for many had died in the forest. Many had vanished into the ground. Dragons and men alike.

This was the boundary line. And yet someone was coming. Someone was coming closer.

Zorag looked toward his people. They had not moved.

Dragon skin was too thick to penetrate when the ground only rumbled because of one person, but Zorag, with his extraordinary sense, could feel the footsteps quite clearly. He could feel them in the most tender places.

And yet he waited.

The footsteps drew ever nearer. And then Zorag saw a man, hidden in shadow behind a tree. Zorag's eye was level with the man's face.

His throat rumbled a bit, in warning to the man, but not so loud that his people were disturbed from their rest. The man looked at him and tilted his head, as if he were not afraid at all of the large beast before him. Zorag did not know whether to be angry or quite glad, for he had missed the humans. Still, this one was about to cross over the boundary line. He could open his mouth and breathe fire and consume this man in little more than a moment. But something held him back.

The man stepped out from the shadows. Zorag saw that he was a handsome man, with deep blue eyes that looked, to him, kind and gentle. They reminded him of the boy he had loved once, back when the dragons began their partnership with the people. And so, quite unnaturally, the dragon bowed.

Was this a long-lost son of the beloved king? Had King Brendon carried a secret that none in the kingdom knew?

Then the man spoke. "I come in peace," he said. "I come to

see you." And Zorag looked in his eyes and knew that the words the man spoke were true, knew that any words the man spoke would be true.

"You should not be here," Zorag said, as quietly as he could manage. "If you are found—"

"I know," the man said. "I, of all people, understand how dangerous it is."

"You, of all people," Zorag said. "And who are you, of all people?"

The man tilted his head to the side again. His hands opened and his arms raised, as if he were in the act of surrendering. "I am the king's son."

Zorag drew back. Not a king's son. A king's son was not welcome here. What could this man with the kind eyes want? How would he betray them? Surely he was sent to destroy the dragons where they had not been destroyed before.

"You," Zorag said, still speaking in a way he could not understand, this careful, low rumble so as not to disturb the others.

"Me," the man said, and he fell to his knees. He fell to his knees and wept, and Zorag watched him. The dragon's heart turned soft and warm, filling with a deep love that he could not deny. "I am sorry," the man said. "I am sorry for what my father did to your people."

Zorag said nothing. He merely waited.

"I am sorry for what my father did to you." The man stood up and walked across the boundary line as if it did not matter in the slightest. He placed his hand on the tender spot on Zorag's neck, where a line of arrows had pierced his father and brought him to his death. Zorag felt the recognition jolt him once more, as he found another rider, so many years after the first.

"I am sorry for this," the man said, and he touched Zorag's broken wing. And then he bowed once more and said, "I am Prince Wendell."

"I am called Zorag," Zorag said.

"Zorag," the prince said, and he smiled. "Well, Zorag."

He said nothing more. He merely climbed on Zorag's back, and Zorag took to the air. It was a choppy flight, to be sure, for it was the first time Zorag had taken to the sky after his wing had been damaged. It had been many years, and his wings did not quite know what to do anymore, even without the injury. But they landed, and the prince stole away, back through the Weeping Woods, without any dragon or man spotting them.

They met again and again and again, the prince climbing on Zorag's back and Zorag taking him all around the land, showing the prince where the dragons were permitted to go and where they were not. It was dangerous for them to fly so close to Fairendale, but Wendell assured him that the people were sleeping, though Zorag flew high so that if there were eyes that happened to look up to the sky, they would not notice the flight of a dragon.

Every night, before they parted, Prince Wendell stroked Zorag's neck and said, "When I am king, you shall be welcome in the land again."

And Zorag began to hope and wait and love again.

But the prince's promise, alas, was never meant to be.

Search

The village people wait, ignoring the calls of the mermaids behind them, who try to warn the people of the castle what is coming for them, but no one has ever, in the history of Fairendale, paid any mind to what mermaids say. One hundred twenty-three people cover the front lawn, up to the stone steps, holding the largest log they could find in the charred forest. They look about at one another as if all asking the same question: Where is Cora? She is their leader, after all. Had they all heard incorrectly? Would she not be here with them? How would they know what to do?

A noise behind them draws their attention, and there is Cora, her red hair streaming loose in the wind, flapping behind her as if on fire. "Now," she says, and they push the log back and ram it into the door and push the log back and ram it into the door, again and again and again, until the castle doors break open and they pile inside. They do not stop to admire the artistry on those ceilings, where famous artists painted until their arms began to shake. They do not stop to examine the marble floors or the portraits of past kings that line the hallway. They merely run toward the throne room, where they know the king to always be. Servants flee as the villagers come, with the log hoisted before them.

They find the throne room barred. They hear the king's voice from within. "This is madness," he says. "What is all this? Who has knocked at my door and broken it?" and they hear, then, the voice of another calming him, Queen Clarion, perhaps, for this is the voice of a woman. And then Cora hears the voice she wants. Prince Virgil. This will be easier than she thought. Cora looks at the village people. "To the kitchens," she orders, and half of them scatter. The rest of them ram the log against the throne room doors. The door does not budge, but they will not give up. And what happens when sixty-two people do not give up when faced with a closed door? Why, it opens.

It opens, dear reader, on quite a comical scene. The people see the king, poking through a hold in the floor. The prince is standing right next to him, as if waiting for his father to sink down inside.

"Go, Father," Prince Virgil says, his voice urgent and high-pitched. He looks as though he is thinking that his father should have let him go first. But his father, you see, was not thinking of his son in those moments of danger. He was only thinking of himself. Prince Virgil urged his mother into the hold first, and so she stands below, pulling on the king's legs. But the king is stuck tight. He can no longer fit inside the hiding place that the castle builder, centuries ago, placed in this throne room for a dangerous moment such as this one, when a king might need a rapid escape route. Our king today is much too large for this hold. He has eaten far too many sweet rolls, and now his legs dangle helplessly below, where who knows what awaits them. This hold has not been used since it was fashioned.

The top side of King Willis juts from the hold, and there is no amount of pushing by Prince Virgil and pulling by Queen Clarion that will make him budge.

Prince Virgil looks on the people, spilling into the throne room, and he looks at his father, stuck tight. His eyes widen. His father says, "Run."

And so he does.

But, alas, there is nowhere in this room to run, not with sixty-two villagers running toward him. He moves to the back and off around the sides, but they have already cornered him. There is a woman, a fast one with flaming red hair he has seen before. Mercy's mother, perhaps? She looks as if Mercy belongs to her. She is the one who reaches him first.

"You will come with us, my dear," she says, and while her words are kind, her eyes are not. He reaches for the talisman he has hung around his neck, but then he remembers that it is a blackbird, and something about a blackbird moves a shiver of fear all the way through him.

Two more men grab Prince Virgil's arms, while his father watches, unable to do anything or go anywhere, not in, not out, because of that enormous belly. The people carry Prince Virgil from the room.

"We will not hurt you," the woman with flaming hair says once they have pulled Prince Virgil from the safety of the castle and begun to drag him down the path toward the village. She says the words so that he will not fight. But, in all honesty, our dear prince does not want to fight, for he is done fighting, and so he goes willingly.

"Where are you taking me?" Prince Virgil says.

"We have prisons of our own in the village," Cora says. She smiles at him, and her face is one long shadow, flickering into a blackbird so momentarily Prince Virgil believes it was only his imagination. Was it only his imagination? We shall have to wait and see.

Prince Virgil shivers again. He does not know what these villagers have planned for him, and neither, in truth, do they, but they do know that what they have caught is precious and valuable to use for negotiation purposes, and so they take him down the road and past the bridge, where a red-haired mermaid taunts them, and then, when she sees Prince Virgil, her eyes grow wide and angry.

Prince Virgil remembers that he has seen this mermaid before. She is not like the others, or at least he does not think she is. He remembers her singing over him once, and he remembers that she saved his life the night he thought he might venture into the woods. It feels so long ago he does not remember if the singing was real or merely a dream. Her eyes meet his. They are fierce and wild. "I will help," she says, and then she dives below the surface.

But what can a mermaid do?

Well, we shall find that out soon enough, dear reader. But for now, let us return to the castle, where King Willis is still stuck tight in a too-narrow passageway.

King Willis was surely not thinking. He should have let his son go first, down into the passageway, and then there would have been some point to his being stuck, would there not? He could have plugged the passageway so that the people could never have reached his son. And now it is too late for a plan as brilliant as this.

In truth, our king was thinking. But he was not thinking of anyone else in the room, only himself. He was thinking of how he needed to escape, for the people had surely come for him. He had been the one to imprison their children, after all. They wanted his head for it. And because he was not willing to die, King Willis forgot all about his son. How will he keep a throne without his son? How will he get his son back without the captain of the king's guard and new men?

Queen Clarion thumps his backside. He can hear her muffled voice. "What is happening?" she says. "What is happening, Willis?" She asks it over and over again, for all King Willis can do is slump over the passageway. He cannot answer his wife. And soon the servants move from their hiding places, for, you see, they did not want to die in the madness, either. They venture inside the throne room to see what might be left. It takes twelve of them pulling and Queen Clarion pushing to get King Willis out of the passage. He pops out with a squelching noise that all the servants, and the queen, pretend not to hear. Queen Clarion climbs out, slipping easily through the passageway with her slender, tall form, though the long, billowing skirt gives her some trouble. She looks around and does not see her son, and it is with a tenderness that blocks their throats that the servants watch their queen collapse right in the middle of the court with sobs that would make any man cry. Any man, that is, except for King Willis.

"Quiet, woman," King Willis says. "I cannot think with all of your noise."

"Our son," Queen Clarion says. She looks up at the king, the lids of her blue eyes lined with red. "Our son is gone. They have taken our son."

"QUIET!" King Willis roars.

The servants do not move, for in their world, quiet means remain as still as possible, so as not to make a sound with mouth or body. Barely even breathe. Queen Clarion, it seems, is the only one brave enough to defy a man as powerful as King Willis, for she is the only one who speaks. "Perhaps we should give their children back," she says. She does not so much as flinch when King Willis turns a heavy hand toward her face.

"I said quiet," he says. "We will not give the children back. That is not part of the plan."

Queen Clarion rises. Grief does strange things to people, if you will remember. Sometimes it makes them brave, as it does Queen Clarion. She is sad enough to take a chance. "But our son," she says. "They have taken our son. Just like we took their sons and daughters. They will want an even trade."

"They will not get an even trade," King Willis says. "We must think of the kingdom."

"We must think of our son," Queen Clarion says. "There is no kingdom without our son."

Oh, how Queen Clarion wishes King Willis were more like his brother. Kind, smart, gracious, helpful, loving. A real man. This shell of a man who stands before her should never have been her husband. None of this would ever have happened.

While these thoughts bounce through our poor queen's head, she does not remain where she is. She moves, instead, toward her husband.

"But the kingdom," King Willis says, and it is as if these words take all the life out of him. He slumps where he stands, his large belly fanning waves of grief. Could it be that he regrets putting his son in danger? Could it be, dear reader, that he does, in fact, love his son? Could it be that we have not known King Willis as well as we thought?

Queen Clarion puts a hand on his arm. She is a woman who can forgive easily, even a man who has made as many mistakes as King Willis. For Queen Clarion knows that forgiveness does not belong to the worthy. It belongs to the giver. And so she can forgive and forgive and forgive, knowing that it does not give this man power over her but gives her power over her own mind and heart.

"We must give them back," she says. "It is the only way."

"It is not the only way." The king and queen look up at this unknown voice. There is a woman, hiding in the shadows at the back of the room. She does not move but merely waits.

King Willis does not recognize her. "Who are you, woman?" he says. "What do you want?"

"Only to help," the woman says. She steps from the shadows. She is dressed in ragged clothes, covered by a dirty apron. She is the castle cook, you see. She is the one who works all day in the kitchen so that King Willis can fill his belly with sweet and delectable morsels. She is a valuable possession for a man like King Willis. She is also not everything she seems, for she has a secret. A shape shifting secret. As you will remember, not many shape shifters exist in this world. As few as six, in fact.

This woman is terribly old, though she looks to be around the age of a grandmother, with plump skin and face and wrinkles in all the right places, as if she is a merry person. Those who work with her know she is not, in fact, merry. Just ask Calvin, who has had his ears boxed for the slightest of reasons. Sometimes for the reason that Cook felt like it. No one in the castle knows that when night falls, she shifts into a bear and rumbles off toward the enchanted wood, where creatures will not hurt a being as large as she can become. No one would be able to tell by looking on her face. No one would be able to see her secret hidden there, for they never venture close enough to Cook to notice the way her chin is just slightly darker with a film fuzz that she never found necessary to remove. Mankind is not so observant. They do not see that her eyes look a bit more animal than most.

Cook bows before the king, agile for one as old as she, though, as said before, she does not look old to their eyes. She is good at hiding who she really is, for no one has ever had any cause to look.

"I am your cook, sire," she says. She looks up, knowing that the king will gaze on her in pleasure.

And she is not disappointed. There is a gleam in the eyes of the king that cannot be mistaken for anything but delight. "Ah," he says. "My cook." He extends his hand. She comes closer, walking across the carpet with feet that make no noise.

"Thank you," she says.

"And what is this other way?" King Willis says. "Pray tell."

"There is someone new to the forest, sire," Cook says.

"Children?" says King Willis, for he remains ever hopeful. He wants this finished just as everyone else does. If they would only hand over the remaining children, it would all be done and over in a day or two, and no one would be the worse, would they? Except, perhaps, the boy who would be killed.

"No," Cook says. "Not children."

"Then who?" King Willis says. He does not even pause to wonder how this woman may know what is in the forest and what is not. Such a dangerous forest is not ever a good place to visit, but he does not consider this. He only considers what she may know.

Queen Clarion looks at the woman with a curiosity that can hardly be contained. But she will save her questions for later.

"A woman," Cook says. "A woman who can help."

"Who is this woman?" King Willis says.

"An Enchantress," Cook says. "A very powerful one. So I have heard."

"And from whom did you hear this?" King Willis says.

"From the animals of the forest," Cook says. She looks at her feet, as if embarrassed. "I have always had a way with animals, sire."

"Are there animals in the forest?" King Willis says. He looks at his wife and back at the woman. "I thought it had burned."

"The animals do not stay gone long," Cook says. "It is their home."

"I see," King Willis says. "And where might I find this woman?"

Cook looks back up at her king. "She lives in a corner of the forest. In a small cottage, surrounded by flowers and trees." Of course it is surrounded by trees. It is, after all, a forest, which only has trees in the first place, but what Cook, who is not so eloquent at speaking, really means is that it is surrounded by trees that are still alive, while most of the trees in the forest remain dead. Though not for long.

"Who will go?" King Willis says. He looks around, searching for his man Sir Greyson. But there is no one, you see. Sir Greyson lost all his men in the battle with the dragons, and King Willis, in a twist of irony, has sent the remaining man off to gather more men in order to protect the castle and its people, just a few moments too late, or perhaps too early, since Sir Greyson might have been able to appeal to the people, since he was one of them. Now King Willis has lost his son.

No one answers the king, of course. They all stare at him with frightened eyes. But there are men still. There are old men and there are very young men, and King Willis finds a very young man, his manservant, in fact, standing nearly behind a chair, trying to remain perfectly invisible. "You," he says.

"Me?" says Garth. His eyes, piercing blue, look frightened and scared, because, dear reader, if you will remember, he is still quite young, not yet a man. His short brown hair is brushed across the right side of his face, almost obscuring those piercing blue eyes and his dark eyebrows. But not quite. In them one can see fear and apprehension, and, yes, quite a bit of pride at having been asked to do the king's important work, so different from his daily tasks of bringing the king sweet rolls and helping him in and out of his throne and down the stairs of the platform.

What those at the castle do not know is that Garth is the oldest of twelve children, some of them down in the dungeons beneath the dungeons and some of them still out missing. Or so he presumes. He does not want to leave his brothers and sisters if they happen to be caught in the dungeons, but perhaps, if they are, instead, wandering, he will be able to find them.

"You will go," King Willis says. "You will find the Enchantress."

"But the woods," Garth says. "There are many dangers inside."

"The woods are burned," King Willis says, waving his hands in dismissal. "There is nothing that will hurt you." He turns to the boy and grins. "At least not if you hurry."

The boy bows down low, as if admitting his defeat, and then he says, "Yes, Your Highness." Queen Clarion raises her eyebrows, for what she hears is "Yes, Your Wideness," and she can see by the flash of merry light in the boy's eyes, which wins over the fear for only a moment, that she was right in her hearing. She looks at King Willis. He does not seem to notice. In spite of the circumstances, she wants to laugh, though her son is missing, though she does not know what the village people will do to him, though she misses him terribly already and cannot bear to think what she will possibly do without him. It is true that in times of grief, people often feel the need to laugh. And yet Queen Clarion remains quiet. She stifles her urge with a gloved hand.

"At the edge of the forest. Near the village," Cook says.

The boy hesitates, for just a moment, looking at Cook, who does not say another word. Her eyes are wide, though, and he knows what that means. There are still dangers in the forest, and she is warning him. He has seen her, sneaking off into the trees and then disappearing into thin air until only a bear remained, lumbering into the shadows. He knows her for what she is. He has never told her secret, and, truth be told, she does not know he knows, but he does not even have time to leverage that knowledge. He only has time to fly, which is what he does, right through the hallways and through the immaculate entryway of the palace and out the front doors. He runs as fast as he can toward the forest, for he will need to catch what little light there is left.

Everyone knows that the most dangerous creatures in the Weeping Woods come out at night. He does not want to know what they are.

At precisely the very moment Garth is racing toward the

forest, down the lawn of the castle and away from the village, the village people are standing beside the fountain's secret entrance. Prince Virgil does not struggle in their arms. He stares at the ground.

"What shall we do with him?" says Bertie, the village baker. "How will we hide him?"

"The king will surely come to get us," another man says. "He will surely have our heads for this treason."

"He has no men to follow us," the woman called Cora says. "He will do nothing." Her eyes flash at the people. "He took our sons and daughters, so we have taken his son."

"This was not part of the plan yet," says Garron, the village gardener.

"Plans change," Cora says. "I saw an opportunity." She smiles at the people. She is a very beautiful woman. Prince Virgil can see the resemblance now. The same green eyes. The same red hair. He wonders if she knows that Mercy is not in the dungeon.

"Mercy is not among those who were found," he says, for a mother should know a thing like this.

Cora looks at Prince Virgil. She does not say anything. But he sees the grief shift in her eyes and turn toward hope, the irises growing brighter, like the grass covering the castle lawn. Why would this information give Cora hope? Is it, perhaps, that she knows her daughter would be safer outside the castle walls?

"She escaped," Cora says.

"Many of them did," Prince Virgil says, and then he remembers the dragons. "But we do not know if they lived."

Cora tilts her head and studies the boy. "What would make you say a thing like that?" she says. "Of course they lived. They have magic."

Prince Virgil swallows hard. He is afraid of this woman. He should not have spoken. "The dragons," he says simply. He leaves it at that, for it is answer enough.

"The dragons did not hurt the children," Cora says. No one asks how she could know this for certain. But her voice says it is fact, not merely opinion.

"If they live, my father will continue searching," Prince Virgil says, for he has seen the truth, the greed, the determination in his father's eyes. Sometimes, you see, plans become obsessions, and King Willis has crossed the line. "He will search until he finds them."

"And what will he do then?" Cora says, but the people have begun to murmur around them, and it is very hard to hear her voice.

"We should set up a search party," Garron says. "We might find them before the king does."

Cora holds up her hand, and the people grow quiet. "Let the

boy speak," she says, and she turns her eyes upon Prince Virgil.

"He searches for a magical boy," Prince Virgil says. "If you could give him to us, perhaps this would all end."

"I do not believe it will end for quite some time," Cora says. "There is no magical boy in Fairendale."

"There is," Prince Virgil says. "A prophetess came. She told my father there was a boy born with magic."

The people murmur again, looking at one another. They have never seen a boy with magic. They have only seen the village girls, out in the streets, using magic to make flowers bloom and shoes dance and toys fly.

"I saw a boy do magic," Prince Virgil says.

The two men who hold him release him now. "No," one of them says. "You must have been mistaken."

"I saw it with my own eyes," Prince Virgil says. "I saw the boy make a wooden puppet fly."

Prince Virgil is free now. No one lays a hand on him. Why would our prince not run from this mob? Why does he remain where he is, answering their questions as if he has nothing in the world better to do. Well, our prince, you see, hopes to sway the people. He hopes they, too, will search for the missing boy so that all of this might be finished. He only wants it to be finished.

"Who is this boy?" Cora says.

"A boy called Theo," Prince Virgil says.

"No," Bertie says. "Theo does not have magic. Arthur would never keep that from us."

"When did you see this magic?" Cora says.

"The day before my father attacked," Prince Virgil says. "I saw him pull a puppet from the sky and then send it flying again."

The people look at each other, erupting into talk.

"Silence!" Cora says. Her voice is sharp and loud. She holds up a hand once more. Her eyes narrow at Prince Virgil. "So you are the reason your father attacked."

"No," Prince Virgil says. "The boy is the reason he attacked."

But it is too late. The people have heard Cora's words.

"My son died," says a woman with a thousand wrinkles around her mud-colored eyes. Her white hair is pulled back at the nape of her neck. "My son died because of you."

Prince Virgil can say nothing, for, in a way, he does feel like it was all his fault. If he were not born without magic, he would not be here at all.

"Leave us," Cora says. The people stare at her for a moment, as if daring to defy her orders. She does not falter in her stance, her eyes meeting theirs with a fire they cannot match. Prince Virgil is impressed when they do precisely what she has said. Their backs turn, and they move toward their houses as one collective unit. "I will figure out a way out of this," Cora calls to their retreating backs. "We will find our children."

She does not say what else is in her mind to say—that they must trust her implicitly to save the children. It will be a circuitous route, to be sure, but she needs their trust to do what has been given her to do.

Prince Virgil looks on this woman who is much more than she seems. He admires her authority. He admires her courage. Perhaps this is why her eyes showed hope when he told her Mercy was not in the castle dungeons. Perhaps Mercy has this same authority, this same courage. He does not know the girl well enough to say, with all certainty, whether she does or does not. But he would like to know. His heart clenches. How he misses his friends. This village. There are so many memories in this village.

And in the space between Cora watching the people return to their homes and when she turns back to Prince Virgil, the boy thinks of his father, what happened only moments ago. He thinks of the throne, of its sparkling jewels, of its promise that does not seem so wonderful now that he is out in the village, back in this place that held the ones he loved. Perhaps it is better that he is here. Perhaps his captivity will free him, in all the ways that matter most.

Prince Virgil studies Cora. Cora studies him. And she is just beginning to open her mouth again when someone shouts, "There is a figure on the king's road," and Cora shoves the prince to the ground, his face flat against the hill beside the fountain. He is quite surprised to feel the ground falling away from him and his body falling down. And before he can even make sense of what is happening, Prince Virgil finds himself in a secret room, dark and chilly. Cora lights candles, and Prince Virgil looks on the tables and chairs, and a bed in the corner. His mouth, of its own volition, drops open. Has this been in the village all along? How?

Shadows flicker in all the corners, pulling their silhouettes long and tall. It is a small room, but the candles make it comfortable. There are no windows, and he sees no door. There will be no way out.

And it is true, dear reader, that there is no way out for a prince, for the room only opens to those who have been given permission to come and go. It is an enchanted room, you see, placed here long ago, before the days of the Good King Brendon, even, when the people had yet to understand dragons and only knew that the lands of Fairendale met the lands of Morad, where it was known that dragons lived. This room was a hideout from the dragons, though it was never used for that purpose. It was not used, in fact, until the days of King Sebastien, when the people found a need to meet in secret.

Prince Virgil is interrupted in his thoughts by the voice of Mercy's mother. "Tell me what you know," she says.

So he does. He tells her about the children in the dungeons beneath the dungeons, about all the ones who are missing, about the tiny shoe one of the king's men found, about how his father ordered the king's men to find the children, and they were all burned up in the fire of dragons.

"They were all burned?" Cora says, and the look on her face tells a story of sorrow. Perhaps the man she saw in the village was not the man she loved so long ago.

"Yes," Prince Virgil says.

"Not a man survived?" Cora says.

"There was one," Prince Virgil says. "The captain."

"Yes," Cora says, and her breath comes out in a whoosh, as if she were holding it in anticipation. "The captain." She raises her eyes to Prince Virgil. "And where is the captain now?"

"My father sent him on a journey to gather more men," Prince Virgil says.

"More men for what?" Cora says.

"For the attack of the dragons," Prince Virgil says.

"The dragons will not attack," Cora says. "They are peaceable enough."

"But my father's men crossed into their land," Prince Virgil says.

And perhaps Cora senses that this boy is frightened of what may happen if the dragons should attack, for she touches the boy's arm, and her eyes grow soft. "Your father's men are all gone," Cora says. "And while that is very, very sad, the dragons will not harm those who have not crossed."

"The children crossed," Prince Virgil says, for there is more in his heart to cause great worry.

"So they did," Cora says. Her eyes grow glassy, far away. Prince Virgil cannot read what is in her eyes now, for the shadows are too large and long. Cora pulls herself back into the room.

"Do you know the children in the dungeons beneath the dungeons?" Cora says.

"No," Prince Virgil says. "I only know that Mercy is not there."

"Did you know my daughter?" Cora says.

"Yes," Prince Virgil says. "I knew her well."

"She is a remarkable girl," Cora says, and her eyes, this time, overflow. It is the first time she has shown her weakness in all these days. To see it makes Prince Virgil feel all the better, for she is demonstrating her humanity, dear reader. It is not our strength, you see, that makes us most human. It is our weakness. And we are all weak in the places where we love. But love is how we know we are alive. It is how we survive. It is our greatest strength.

Cora glances at the wall behind Prince Virgil. She does not look at him when she says, "I must keep you here."

"I understand," Prince Virgil says, for she has won him over with her humanity. He has seen something in her face, something that reminds him of his mother's kindness. Though one might argue that Cora and her storied past do not tell of kindness so much as ruthlessness, it is clear to Prince Virgil that kindness is the pen that wrote it all. And we, too, shall see that soon enough.

Cora looks at Prince Virgil for a moment, two, three. He tries his best to meet her gaze, but those green eyes feel as if they might peel away all his layers and see all the way inside his heart, and so he turns his back to her. And then Cora says, "You are a good one," so he must, he must, oh, he must look back, for perhaps she has seen something that he has not known existed. "I can see," she says, as if she hears the very question that escapes from his heart. "You did not think so for a time. But we are going to keep you good."

And then he feels a great wrenching in his body, as if someone is flattening him beneath the heaviest weight he has ever carried. It is nothing like the weight of the mind but is physical and demanding and frightening. Perhaps he screams. Perhaps he does not. He only remembers looking into the eyes of this woman called Cora and hearing a fluttering sound and knowing nothing more.

Garth searches the forest as long as he dares. But he finds nothing. There is nothing in the forest but burned trees and the smell of death. He looks everywhere, all along the boundary between the village and the forest, and, in a burst of fear, rushes inside, to the surprise of the village people who watch him. He does not go deep, of course, for Cook said he would find a house just inside. And, truth be told, he is frightened of what the forest holds.

But there is nothing. Nothing for him to see, nothing for him to report. He does not know what he will do. He will surely be dismissed, and what then? He will not be able to ensure that his brothers and sisters in the dungeons beneath the dungeons are fed and cared for. He will not be able to slip his own provisions into the hands of the boy called Calvin. He will not be able to help them escape.

He will, instead, return to his mother, who was not among the line of villagers watching him when he stole into the woods, for she rarely comes out of her home. It is too quiet a house, now that her twelve children have gone. It carries a great loneliness, one he cannot even bear to meet once a week anymore. He sends his word from the village instead, using pigeons, as the royal family and castle workers have done for centuries. His mother does not write back.

He must find that hidden house. He must. He must not be dismissed from the service of the king. He must not leave his brothers and sisters to their fate.

But the boy searches until the sun has only the smallest sliver left in the sky, and the night creatures begin calling. So he races back out, as fast as he has ever run before in his life. He collapses on the grass just outside the border. He lies there a very long time, looking at the forest, wishing that something would magically, wonderfully appear before his very eyes.

And then, finally, he returns to the castle with his disappointing news that may very well end in a dismissal. But when he returns to the castle, he finds that the king is indisposed, a belly ache, Queen Clarion says, and he has been locked in his chambers for some time. He does not even want his manservant.

"Go," Queen Clarion says. She touches his face. "Go rest for the eve."

"Thank you, my lady," he says, with a bow.

"Garth," Queen Clarion says before he has risen from his bow. Her voice is soft and gentle. "Did you find anything?"

He shakes his head. "No, my lady," he says. "I am sorry."

"Do not be sorry," Queen Clarion says. "It is better that the children remain hidden." Her eyes turn glassy. "And did you see my son?"

In truth, Garth was not looking for Prince Virgil at all, but how can he tell this woman, this woman who heard him call the king Your Wideness and smothered a laugh at the audacity of it, that he did not feel any kind of concern for her son? So he does what any boy in his position would do when faced with a beautiful queen and a difficult question. He lies.

"No, my lady," Garth says. "I did not see him."

It is not so very big a lie, I am sure you would agree, for it is true that Garth did not see Prince Virgil. It is also true, however, that he was not looking for the prince. Might he have seen something if he had been looking? Well, we know he would not. Prince Virgil is tucked away in the secret room. But Garth does not know this.

Queen Clarion's eyes spill, but she does not say more. She merely nods and turns around with a swish of her skirts. Garth watches the queen walk the entire length of the hall and turn around a corner. Only then does he return to his bedchambers and revise his plan.

He will set the children free and he will find the prince. Everyone will live happily ever after.

Oh, dear Garth. If only planning could make it so.

Flight

Not long after their rides began in the dark of night, the prince came to Zorag on an evening darker than the rest, and said, "I must flee."

Zorag looked on his prince and felt the wrenching in his heart. Must he lose another rider?

"My father has banished me from the kingdom," Prince Wendell said.

"Your father," Zorag said. "Why would he do such a thing?" He said the words with all the hatred he felt inside.

Prince Wendell touched Zorag's cheek. "He is a good man," he said. "He has had a hard life, and he does not quite know what to do with all of that. Power can turn a man cruel."

Yes. Zorag knew all about what power could do in a man. He saw it before the good King Brendon, after all. He had seen it in many a man, had even begun to notice it in Blindell, as the dragons of Morad began to pay more and more attention to the young dragon and his need for revenge.

"And why has your father banished you?" Zorag said.

Prince Wendell shook his head. "It matters not," he said. "It matters only that I must leave at once."

"Stay with us," Zorag said.

"It is too dangerous," Prince Wendell said. "Your people will not like a human living among you."

Zorag said nothing, though the dragons carried a secret, too.

"I must go," Prince Wendell said.

"Then I shall take you," Zorag said.

Prince Wendell shook his head. "No," he said. "It is too dangerous for you."

"Then why is it you have come?" Zorag said.

"To say goodbye," Prince Wendell said.

"I must see you to safety," Zorag said, for he did not want to say goodbye to this human he loved.

"No," Prince Wendell said. "I cannot let you risk it."

"I cannot let you risk a journey on foot," Zorag said. "You will never travel fast enough."

Prince Wendell did not argue. He merely dipped his head. "Very well," he said. He climbed on his dragon's back.

Zorag took to the sky, on this last night that he would carry a rider on his back, for this time he would surely never love a human being as he had loved Prince Wendell.

And when he had landed with Prince Wendell in a grassland between Lincastle and Eastermoor, he returned to Morad to grieve in solitude.

Night

King Willis is in his royal chamber when the news comes to him of his manservant's return. He is indisposed, that much is true, but that does not mean he does not wish to hear of what the manservant found. So he rings the bell beside his bed, the one that leads directly to Garth's room, and it takes the boy only minutes to reach him.

As soon as Garth enters his bedchambers, King Willis knows it is not with good news that the boy has returned. Garth stares at the floor.

"Well?" the king says. "Tell me, what did you find?"

Garth shakes his head. "I found nothing," he says.

The king growls. "You found nothing?" he says. "How is it that you found nothing?"

"There is no house," Garth says.

"There is no house," King Willis says. "Tell me, how is it that there is no house, when Cook says there is a house?"

"I do not know," Garth says. "Perhaps I should fetch Cook."

"Yes," King Willis says. "Perhaps you should." It is quite clear that the king is not happy. Garth scuttles from the room and returns, moments later, with Cook, who has not yet put on her bear skin, for she, too, was waiting for the boy's return.

"The boy has found nothing," King Willis says. He is sitting in his bed. His stomach twists and turns, but he tries his best to ignore it. "Tell me how it is that the boy has found nothing." He is looking at Cook.

She shuffles a large foot. "It is an invisible house," Cook says.

"An invisible house," King Willis says. "You sent the boy looking for an invisible house?" Garth looks at Cook, as if asking the very same thing.

"Children can often see what we cannot," Cook says. "I thought, perhaps, he might see it."

"But he is not a child," King Willis says. He squints his eyes, but his eyesight is poor. So he simply says, "Or maybe he is."

"No," Garth says. "No, I am not a child." He gives Cook a look, one that says, *Please do not tell him*, and Cook does not. King Willis does not notice what passes between the two.

Instead, the king turns to Cook. "Why did I not send you instead," he says, "so that you might find the invisible house?"

"You would not have had supper," she says. Her bushy

eyebrows draw low over her dark eyes.

"Yes. Very well," King Willis says. "Quite right." He has nothing more to say, no other ideas, for his stomach, you see, is quite knotted up.

"Perhaps I might go in the morning," Cook says.

"Yes," the king says. "Yes. You will. After breakfast."

"Very well, sire," Cook says.

She will, in fact, go this very night. She will find nothing. The Enchantress, you see, has hidden her house from even shape shifters now. She saw the bear the first night. She could not risk a spy, for she has the treasure of Hazel, and she must make sure it all remains hidden until just the right moment.

If the king were to search for months, sending any person he might spare for the day, no one would find even a trace of the two houses, sitting in the woods, hiding the very children the king so desperately desires.

The king dismisses Garth and Cook to their beds, for it is very late.

No one sleeps this night.

Arthur is huddled up tight, trying to sleep on a rock, but his back is old, and he does not much like sleeping in such a position, for it is not really sleep at all, only dozing and waking and dozing and waking. He has felt the torture of every day, without his wife and children, and every night it is more pronounced, for there are no bodies to warm him inside this cave. There is no rest for him in this land. It is true that he had thought to fare better than this, when the dragons took him away, but the dragons are a difficult people, and he does not know in the slightest what he might do to walk on their good side.

And then, just as Arthur has drifted into another patch of light sleep, the shadow dragon Arthur saw the one and only time Zorag visited him, lands on the ledge. Arthur cannot remember his name, but the dragon does not hesitate to tell him.

"I am called Blindell," he says. "We met two days past."

"Yes," Arthur says. "I remember."

In the last two days, it has been random dragons delivering his food, keeping him "safe and comfortable," they say in voices that sound anything but happy about this charge. And while Arthur is grateful that the dragons have taken it upon themselves to feed another person when most of them are starving themselves, he does not quite feel he has been kept safe and comfortable. His back hurts too badly to claim that. And he has asked each dragon if he might speak with Zorag again, yet Zorag has not come.

Arthur stands now, but it is slowly. The dragon notices.

"Humans are not used to sleeping on rock," Blindell says.

"No," Arthur says. "Though at least I am alive. I am grateful for that."

The young dragon lets out a syncopated roar that must be a laugh. "Yes," he says. "At least you are alive." He looks at the cave where Arthur has been hidden these days past, and then he says, "I might be able to find something more comfortable than rock. So you might find some sleep."

"That would be very kind," Arthur says. He looks at Blindell with a face that exposes none of the distrust he feels for this dragon. And then he says, "And what would you have of me?" for Arthur knows as well as anyone that dragons like Blindell do nothing without something in return.

"The truth," Blindell says. "That is all."

"The truth about what?" Arthur says. His heart beats faster, though one would not be able to tell, from the blank look on his face, that he has anything at all to hide.

"The truth about the children and this war," Blindell says.

Arthur spreads his hands. "I have told all I know," Arthur says. "You were there." He is speaking, of course, of the meeting he had with Zorag, when Blindell hung about in the shadows.

Blindell dips his head, as if nodding in dragon-speak. "I know," he says. His voice is a rumble, higher pitched than

Zorag's. Though his eyes look playful, Arthur knows very well how dangerous a dragon like this one can be. He has heard them called Furies or some such, for they move in and out of rages like a day moves in and out of light. In their worst moments, they use their spikes, all along their back and at the end of their wings and atop their head, to run through men. "I wish to hear it again," Blindell says.

"Very well," Arthur says. He is a wise man, and he has seen the wild flicker of anger in Blindell's eyes. He is not one to make a dragon like this one angry, for if he has any hope of living, he must live to please him. So he tells Blindell what the dragon wants to hear.

When Arthur is finished, Blindell says, "So you are really fighting for the children?"

"We are fighting to protect the children," Arthur says. "And we are not really fighting at all. We are only running. Only…"

"You have lost your children now," Blindell says.

"Yes," Arthur says. "Yes, I have lost all the children." He feels a deep sadness come over him. First his son and now is wife and daughter. He has no way of knowing whether they are alive or dead. He may never see them again, and this is something that can weigh heavily on a man. Though Arthur holds hope, he also knows reality. No man can survive a burning forest, and even if, by some miracle, they did, what would they do then?

Where would they go for safety? Without him, would they be able to escape?

"You are concerned," Blindell says, "that your children are dead."

"They are not all my children," Arthur says. "Although they were." It is not so easy to explain how a man loves children who were not born to him. But Arthur felt responsible for these. He felt love for them.

"I understand," Blindell says. "I was not Zorag's child. But I am his."

"Just so," Arthur says.

"What if I told you they were still alive?" Blindell says.

"I would beg you all to let me go," Arthur says. He does not even hesitate to say the words.

"And that answer would be no," Blindell says. "My cousin has no intention of letting you go."

"Then I would try to escape," Arthur says. Sadness, followed by hope, followed by resolution, can often make a man quite bold. Arthur is, in fact, feeling reckless. He must escape if the children are alive, you see. He must protect them from the dangers that wait. He must not lose a single one of them.

"You would not escape," Blindell says. "The dragons watch your every move."

"But I must protect them," Arthur says. "I would try at all

costs."

"They are protected for now," Blindell says. He turns toward the dragon lands and lifts his head high, standing straight and enormous next to Arthur. Arthur must tilt his head all the way back to see the dragon's face, and even then, he cannot see the eyes well enough to read them. Has the dragon just told him that his children are, in fact, safe? That they are, in fact, alive?

"So the children," Arthur says. "They are alive?"

"They are alive," Blindell says. "But there is still a war."

"It is not a war so much," Arthur says. "It is a search."

Blindell turns on him, dropping his face to Arthur's so that Arthur can see, clearly and distinctly, how fiery his red eyes can become. The dragon's throat glows. Arthur ducks a bit. "There is a war," Blindell says. "It began when the people of Fairendale stepped across our lands." He lifts his head again, taking with it the danger of fire. Arthur stands straight once more. "My cousin just cannot see it."

"Is it so important a war?" Arthur says, at the risk of getting swallowed up in a fire that still glows around Blindell's throat.

Blindell does not say anything for a time. "These are the people who stole a village of children," he says, finally. "You do not even know what they will do to those children. Do you?" He turns a sideways glance on Arthur. Arthur reads contempt in the dragon's eyes.

Arthur shakes his head. "No," he says. "I would hope they would let all the innocent children go."

"But your son," Blindell says. "What of him?"

Arthur shakes his head. "Sometimes one must sacrifice for the good of others," he says.

"And how might you convince the good king that he should let the innocent children go?" Blindell says. "When they have run for so long. Is it not treason to run from the command of a king?"

Arthur does not answer. Blindell goes on. "Perhaps you will appeal to the king's kindness. Perhaps you will ask nicely and he might agree. Perhaps you will offer your son and your daughter."

No, Arthur would never do that.

"Men do not listen to reason," Blindell says. "Not when it comes to power. Not when it comes to winning a war." He bends down low, toward Arthur. The glow in his throat has faded. "Your king is exactly like his father before him. He will stop at nothing, not even the death of innocents, to get what he wants."

Arthur looks into Blindell's red eyes. They are full of hate and anger and something more. Yes. Something more. Sorrow.

"Men do not need war," Arthur says. "Men need only to listen to one another."

"You are a fool," Blindell says. "I thought I could help you."

This, of course, gives Arthur pause. What might Blindell do

to help a peaceful man like Arthur? What might he propose? What might he orchestrate?

"How might you help me?" Arthur says. "You would help me escape?"

"I would help you find your children," Blindell says. "I would help you save them. I would destroy the king and his men. There are many among the dragons who see it my way." He moves his head off to the left. "Not my cousin's."

"Destruction is not the way," Arthur says. "My children would not want the kingdom of Fairendale destroyed for their sake. It is their home, after all. I could not do it."

Blindell glares at him, his eyes narrowed and glowing and, though the brightest red Arthur has ever seen, cold. They send a shiver down his aching back. "Then you all lose," the dragon says and lifts toward the sky, his wings beating wind onto Arthur's face.

Arthur is, once more, left alone. There is nothing more to do but lie down and try to sleep. So this is what he does, though there is no sleep waiting for him this night.

And if he were to look, he might very well see that there is someone else in this cave who does not sleep, someone who has been here all along, watching him, waiting, until the right time for stepping from shadows.

Don't miss out on the next Fairendale adventure!

Will the dragons join the fight for innocent children? Find out in Book 6: *The Mysterious Separation*.

A Short History of the Weeping Woods

**From the journal of Dale Enderling
Explorer**

I discovered The Woods (I have no other name to call them. I am all out of names at this point, and these woods do not particularly distinguish themselves from all the others as I walk through them) on my way south through Fairendale. I must reach warmer lands. The cold is not good for my old bones.

I have seen many unknown creatures, but they do not disturb my wanderings. In fact, I have not had a good look at any of them, for they are quick to hide themselves as I venture through. I am glad for this, for I have seen many creatures in my other wanderings, and they have been quite frightening. Is it better to see the dangers or for those dangers to remain hidden?

This remains to be seen, I suppose. I hurry on.

But I must stop and admire the trees in these woods. They are quite extraordinary, and here are my observations, along with names for the three types of trees I have found to reside here in The Woods.

Dwarfed Giant Sequecas: These trees are magnificent. There are not many here, and they are not so tall as they were in the land of Rosehaven, but they are the same kind of tree. I know them for their very large trunks, though these in The Woods would only require one or two people to wrap their arms around them, where those in the land of Rosehaven require thirty or more.

The trunks themselves are rough and brown, a golden sort of brown. The leaves are like fronds of a plant, slightly spiky. They are bright green. Some of them have brown cones, and I suspect there are creatures living in them, but I did not disturb any.

At their tops, these trees form a sort of cove, presiding over the other trees, which I shall detail below.

This particular tree is not abundant in The Woods, but merely scattered throughout.

Aslin tree: Deeper in The Woods are the trees I have named Aslin. They have smooth, white bark and small black notches on them that look as though they have sustained a bit of dragon fire in their day. I suspect there are dragons living very near here. I only hope I do not have to meet them.

The leaves of the Aslin tree scale a variety of shades, from pale yellow-green to a darker green. They are shaped like tear drops and are veined in remarkable ways, as though an artist painted a jagged masterpiece on a leaf.

These trees grow very closely together, which thickens the woods and blots out the sun.

Caphonwood tree: This tree variety is, by far, the most populous in The Wood. The branches and trunks are thick brown and gnarled. Some of them twist up to the sky or out at the sides. Some of them even weave majestically toward the ground. The tops of these trees leave little room for light, their leaves and branches are so abundant.

Upon careful examination, one could imagine, in the roughened and notched bark of this tree's trunk, a face. Perhaps

I have found some dryads. Or perhaps I am only an old man who grows tired and so finds himself given to fancies, rather than rationality. This is more likely the case.

As I said, I have seen no animals on my travels, but I can always feel them watching me. I hope they continue watching and do not find me a tasty treat.

I must sign off. It is time for sleep.

An addition from author L.R. Patton

Dale Enderling named these woods "The Woods," but after the Great Battle, in which King Sebastien stole the throne of Fairendale from the Good King Brendon, these woods became known as the Weeping Woods. This is mostly due to the trees. The trees that Enderling called Caphonwood trees became hereafter weepingwood trees. Their branches still twisted and turned in every which direction, but it is their leaves that have undergone the most significant transformation. They droop toward the ground, like the waters of a fountain.

It is said that the creatures of the Weeping Woods became much darker and more dangerous after the quest of King Sebastien, though that has not yet been proven as fact. It is also rumored that those who were killed in the Weeping Woods during the Great Battle still haunt it, in one way or another. This, too, has not yet been proven as fact.

At any rate, it might still be wise to avoid the Weeping Woods, as every child in Fairendale is warned at some point or another.

Survival Skills of the Fittest

By King Willis
King Superior of Fairendale

When one is a king, one must protect himself at all costs. That is what my father always told me, and I believe it is exceptional advice.

A king must rule a land, after all. What is a land without its king?

As such, a king must, at all costs, be preserved. This means that when people storm the castle, a king must be first into the protection space. This means that when armies march against the land, the king must be the most diligently protected. This means that if dragons attack the land, the king must be well hidden and well protected, in order to preserve the dignity and the existence of the land.

If you should ever find yourself a king (not the king of Fairendale, of course. You will not have this throne. Of that you can be certain), here are my own survival skills of the fittest.

1. Command the people to do as you say.

This is how you get to be the fittest, you see? Everyone will be afraid of defying you because you are the one in charge. You are the one with the power to order their execution. So you must assert yourself as the person in charge, at all times, including in the midst of battle.

2. If you find your castle under siege, run.

You may not be able to run as fast as I can, but you must at least try. You will have to run because there is no telling what crazed people will do to their king. Power is intoxicating to the common man. Everyone wants to be a king. Everyone will want what you have, and you must flee from them or they will take from you what you have worked so hard to gain.

3. If you cannot escape by running, look out for yourself first.

You are, as we have already established, the most important person in the castle. The only reason Queen Clarion made it to the hiding hole in the throne room before I did is because she was nearer to it and our son urged her to climb inside it. She, of course, slipped inside gracefully, as she does everything. I thought I might slip in gracefully as well, but, well, you know what happened. Someone did not make a wide enough hiding hole.

4. Learn how to wriggle.

This is, alas, what did me in. I never properly learned how to wriggle. I am confident that I could have slid down that hiding hole if I had only learned the proper technique for wriggling. Make sure your education is not as incompetent as mine. I will make sure to teach my son how to wriggle…if the village people will ever return him.

5. If all else fails, properly defend yourself.

I never did learn how to defend myself. I never learned how to wield a sword properly or how to fist fight or how to ride a horse. It is imperative that every future king learns these important aspects of royal living.

6. Be a king.

If you are a king, you are assured survival. You are the fittest. You are the highest of the land. No one dares mess with you when you are a king, unless, of course, your village people go a little mad, as mine have done.

With proper education, proper practice, and proper strategic thinking, you, too, can become one of the fittest, as long as it is far outside the land of Fairendale.

This land is mine.

A One-Sided Conversation with a Parent in Fairendale

By Your Narrator
Storyteller

My child, I must tell you one thing about this land that is more important than any other: Do not venture inside the Weeping Woods when it is dark.

In fact, do not venture inside them at all.

Because fairies exist in the woods. These fairies will carry you off to a land where you will never see me again. They are not the beautiful creatures you have likely heard about in happier stories. They are a hungrier sort who feed off the fear of the children they take to Never Land in order to continue their existence.

Never Land? It is a dark and lonely place.

Yes, they live in the cones of the trees inside the Weeping Woods, and if you wake them, there is no way out.

No, my child, unfortunately there is not always a way out.

And if you think the fairies are bad, well, you should see some of the other creatures in this wood.

What do these other creatures look like? Why, we do not even have the words to describe them.

How do you survive in the Weeping Woods? You do not.

So do not ever go inside them. Are we clear?

Good. Now please eat your dinner before it grows cold.

The Royal Family of Fairendale

King Willis: The current king of Fairendale. Has a deep love for sweet rolls, and it shows in his, well, wideness.

Queen Clarion: The current queen of Fairendale. Is underestimated by her husband, but we shall see just how powerful she is soon enough.

Prince Virgil: Son of King Willis and Queen Clarion, best friend of Theo. Prefers rye bread with melted butter to sweet rolls, depending on the day.

King Sebastien: Deceased king of Fairendale, exception to the line of boys who tried to steal thrones and were, upon failing at their quest, forever banished to sail the Violet Sea. Was killed by a blackbird.

The Villagers of Fairendale

Arthur: Village furniture maker and magic instructor to girls who possess the gift of magic. Is a bit reckless but always manages to come out on the other side—though one is not always assured it will be so.

Maude: Arthur's wife. Bakes spectacular pumpkin sugar cookies. Prefers caution to reckless abandon.

Hazel: Daughter of Arthur and Maude, twin of Theo. Cares for the village sheep and can even, amazingly, understand them.

Theo: Son of Arthur and Maude, twin of Hazel. Finishes his chores early so he can sit in on magic lessons.

Mercy: Daughter of Cora, best friend of Hazel. Prefers spectacular acts of magic to "boring" ones.

Cora: Mother of Mercy, widow, shape shifter. A woman who moves.

Garron: The town gardener. Talks to plants as though they can hear him. Has three sons: 12-year-old twins and a 13-year-old.

Bertie: The town baker. Enjoys showing off his air-kneading skills for the children.

Staff of Fairendale Castle

Garth: Page for King Willis, the oldest of twelve children. Sometimes calls King Willis "Your Wideness."

Cook: One of the few shape shifters in the land. Shape shifts into a bear. Is highly annoyed by her assistant, Calvin.

Calvin: An orphan who began working as Cook's assistant instead of traveling to live with distant relatives in Ashvale—and so did not perish in the Fire Mountain that claimed the entire population of Ashvale many years ago. Tasked with feeding the prisoners in the dungeons beneath the dungeons.

Sir Greyson: Captain of the king's guard. Receives medicine, which keeps his mother alive, in exchange for his service to the king. Carries a magical sword that cannot be lifted by any but him.

Sir Merrick: Second in command to Sir Greyson.

Important Prophets

Aleen: A prophetess who is one hundred forty-two years old, from the kingdom of White Wind. Wears ebony skin and what appears to be a collection of snakes for hair (though it is not).

Yerin: A prophet who is one hundred forty-two years old, from the wild woodland between Lincastle and Eastermoor. Has white hair that makes the dark of the dungeons where he is imprisoned a bit less dark.

Dragons of Morad

Zorag: King of the dragons of Morad. Lost his parents in the Great Battle, when King Sebastien stole the throne from the Good King Brendon. Would like nothing more than peace.

Blindell: Zorag's cousin, raised as the dragon king's son. Lost his parents in the Great Battle, when King Sebastien stole the throne from the Good King Brendon. Would like nothing more than revenge.

Larus: One of the elder dragons of Morad, male. Counselor to Zorag.

Malera: One of the elder dragons of Morad, female.

Counselor to Zorag.

The lost 12-year-old children of Fairendale

Ursula

Chester

Charles

Thumbelina (known as Lina among the children)

Minnie

Jasper

Frederick

Ruby

Martin

Oscar

Homer

Anna

Aurora

Rose

Edgar

Harriet (known as Hattie among the children)

Isabel (known as Izzy among the children)

Ralph

Dorothy

Julian

Tom Thumb

Philip

About the Author

While she has never possessed the gift of magic, L.R.'s teachers claimed she had a gift for words, which one might agree is quite like a gift of magic. Bringing a story to life that did not exist before is very much like transforming an old shoe into a dish towel. L.R. feels quite honored that she was given this gift and hopes to use it to encourage other young writers to discover their own gifts, for what is the world without words and stories?

L.R. is the queen of her castle in San Antonio, TX. She lives with her king and her six young princes, who daily give her inspiration for more grand tales of magic and adventure.

www.lrpatton.com

A Note From L.R.

I hope you've enjoyed reading this book from the annals of Fairendale's history. The world of Fairendale has been a lovely world to create, and I've had fun sketching maps, re-reading fairy tales and thinking, endlessly, about characters and their plights—because a series like this one takes lots and lots of time and hard work. But because it's always been my dream to create a fantasy world and share it with my readers, I knew it was something I had to do. (So, you see, dreams really do come true.)

If you have any questions about Fairendale or simply want to send me a note to tell me who your favorite character is or what kinds of extras you'd like to see me release in the future (a *Creatures of the Violet Sea* is coming soon!), email me at lr@lrpatton.com. I always enjoy hearing from my young readers.

Please consider leaving (or ask your parent to leave) a review of this book wherever you bought it. Reviews help get books into the hands of potential new readers, which is incredibly important for authors like me. And don't forget to pick up your free bonus materials when you stop by my web site! (www.lrpatton.com)

Thank you so much for supporting my work.

In love,

L.R.

Enjoy more stories from the magical Fairendale series:

LRPatton.com/Fairendale

Starter Library

Once upon a time...

The kingdom of Fairendale used to be the most peaceful in all the lands. Its people had never held a weapon before. And now they must, for the sake of the land. For the sake of their families. For the sake of their beloved king.

Read all about the king who had no heir, the girl who had magic, the dragon they loved, and the battle that changed everything in Fairendale's short story prequel, "The Good King's Fall."

Get it FREE, along with bonus materials "The Magical Rules of Fairendale" and "The Lands of Fairendale," for a limited time.

To get your FREE bonus materials, visit *
LRPatton.com/goodking

*Must be 13 or older to be eligible